Bladys of the Stewponey by Sabine Baring-Gould

Sabine Baring-Gould was born on January 28th, 1834. The family had its own manor house at Lew Trenchard on a three-thousand-acre estate, in Devon, England,

His bibliography is immense. 1200 items at a minimum including the hymns 'Onward Christian Soldiers' and 'Now the Day Is Over'.

The family spent much of his childhood travelling in Europe and he was educated mainly by private tutors although he spent two years King's College School in London and a few months at Warwick Grammar School. Here he contracted a bronchial disease that was to plague him throughout his life.

In 1852 he gained entrance to Cambridge University, earning a Bachelor of Arts in 1857, and then a Master of Arts in 1860 from Clare College, Cambridge.

As early as 1853 he had decided to become ordained. In 1864, after his education and several years teaching, he took Holy Orders.

He became the curate at Horbury Bridge in West Riding. Here he met Grace Taylor, the daughter of a mill hand, aged fourteen. During the next few years they fell in love. His vicar, John Sharp, arranged for Grace to live with relatives in York to learn middle-class manners. Baring-Gould, meanwhile, relocated to become perpetual curate at Dalton, near Thirsk.

He and Grace were married in 1868 at Wakefield. Their marriage lasted until her death 48 years later, and the couple had 15 children.

Baring-Gould became the rector of East Mersea in Essex in 1871. In 1872 his father died and he inherited the family estates which included the gift of the living of Lew Trenchard parish. Upon its vacancy in 1881, he took the post, becoming parson as well as squire.

He wrote many novels, his usual writing position was whilst standing, including The Broom-Squire set in the Devil's Punch Bowl (1896), Mehalah and Guavas, the Tinner (1897), a collection of ghost stories, and a 16-volume The Lives of the Saints.

His studies in folklore resulted in The Book of Were-Wolves (1865), a frequently cited study of lycanthropy.

The popular work Curious Myths of the Middle Ages, published in two parts, in 1866 and 1868. Each of the book's twenty-four chapters deals with one medieval superstition, its variants and history.

Grace died in 1916. He had carved on her headstone: Dimidium Animae Meae ("Half my Soul").

Sabine Baring-Gould died on January 2nd, 1924 at Lew Trenchard. He was buried next to Grace.

Index of Contents

INTRODUCTORY NOTE

This story is set in England in the days when women were regarded as having a low status, highwaymen and murder were common and people were executed for trivial offences.

The novel is based on two historical events:

The first of these was the last public execution by burning in England which took place in Shrewsbury in 1789. The horror of the scene is graphically enhanced by the description of the tolling bell:

"St Mary's bell boomed, sending throbs of sound overhead that beat against the walls of the house in one street, and came back muffled in recoil."

The second event was where a young lady had to endure the shame of being the prize at a bowling contest. This is described as follows:

"O yes! O yes! O yes! This is to give notice that this 'ere evening, at six o'clock, at Stewponey, there will be a grand champion match at bowls on the green. The prize to be Bladys Rea, commonly called Stewponey Bla. Admittance one shilling. 'Arf-a-crown inner ring, and ticket admits to the 'oly function, by kind permission of the proprietor, in the Chapel of Stourton Castle. At six o'clock per-cise. No 'arf-price. Children and dogs not admitted."

The heroine of the novel, Bladys Rea, of Spanish extraction, has to undergo a mock marriage under duress, performs an act of kindness to a woman sentenced to death and is later falsely accused and tried for murder herself.

PREFACE

I went to Shropshire with the purpose of working up into a romance the story of Wild Kynaston the Outlaw. I halted on my way at Kinver, with a very old friend. After breakfast on the morning following my arrival, he said to me, "What shall we do to-day? Whither shall we go? Would you like to see our Troglodites?"

"Troglodites!" echoed I. "I have seen the cave dwellings, and cave dwellers in Southern France; surely we have none in England."

"Come and see," he answered. He took me that day to Holy Austin Rock, and we investigated the dwellings there; then, in the afternoon, we went to "The Stewponey," and on to the Rock Tavern, with its subterranean cellars and stables, and then went on to Meg-a-Fox Holes, and the extraordinary assembly of cave dwellings, still occupied, at Drake's Lowe.

All the way my friend, who knew the neighbourhood from childhood, who was, in fact, hereditarily connected with it, yarned to me of the old days when the Irish Road was haunted by highwaymen, when the Stewponey Inn was a great resting-place on the way, when the redoubted Poulter, alias Baxter, was head of a gang of highwaymen who employed the caves as places of refuge and for the concealment of goods, when Lydia Norris of the Rock Inn and her husband were always ready to swear an alibi when required, should a highwayman be "nabbed."

From Kinver I went on to Shrewsbury, and there, in the Library, read in the local Notes and Queries how that the last case of burning for petty treason took place at Shrewsbury in 1790. Thence I went on to Ness Cliff, and saw Kynaston's Cave, where lived he and his horse when he was outlawed.

Now, I cannot describe how it was, but somehow the several scenes and circumstances arranged themselves in my mind about another germ idea from that on which I intended to found my story. Twenty years ago, travelling by night from Freiburg to Brussels I read Maurus Jokai's "Beautiful Michal," and now the idea worked out in that story by the great Hungarian writer started to renewed life in these surroundings and displaced Wild Kynaston. I could not get back to my original idea, and taking the idea of an executioner seeking a wife where he and his profession were not known, the idea that lies at the root of Jokai's story, I allowed it to re-shape itself, in fresh scenes, with fresh developments, and fresh characters. The idea originally came to Jokai, I believe, from the tradition of the origin of the noble family of Schelm, just as in his "Nameless Castle" he has used the curious story of "The Mysterious Inmates of Schloss Eishausen" in Bülaus' Geheime Geschichten (Leipzig, 1851.

I suppose every romance grows out of some occurrence of which one has heard, or read, or with which one has oneself been associated, but it moulds itself afresh in one's brain. This is how the story now presented to the reader came into being. Doubtless every writer of romance knows how that, when once an idea has laid hold of him, and has associated itself with certain scenes, he is powerless to alter its life and development It must take its course, and drags him after it It was so with me.

S. BARING-GOULD.

CHAPTER I. — OYEZ!

In a faded and patched blue coat, turned up with red, the bellman of Kinver appeared in the one long street of that small place—if we call it a town we flatter it, if we speak of it as a village we insult it—and began to ring outside the New Inn.

A crowd rapidly assembled and before the crier had unfolded the paper from which he proposed reading, an ape of a boy threw himself before him, swinging a turnip by the stalk, assumed an air of pomposity and ingenious caricature of the bellman, and shouted:

"O yes! O yes! O yes! Ladies and gents all, I gives notice that you, none of you, ain't to believe a word Gaffer Edmed says. O no! O no! O no!"

"Get along, you dratted jackanapes!" exclaimed the crier testily, and, striking the youth in the small of his back with the bell handle, sent him sprawling. Then, striding forward, he took position with a foot on each side of the prostrate urchin, rang again, and called:

"O yes! O yes! O yes! This is to give notice that this 'ere evening, at six o'clock, at Stewponey, there will be a grand champion match at bowls on the green. The prize to be Bladys Rea, commonly called Stewponey Bla. Admittance one shilling. 'Arf-a-crown inner ring, and ticket admits to the 'oly function, by kind permission of the proprietor, in the Chapel of Stourton Castle. At six o'clock per-cise. No 'arf-price. Children and dogs not admitted."

From the door of the New Inn issued Thomas Hoole, the landlord, in his shirt sleeves.

Thomas Hoole was a bit of a wag and a crumb of a poet. On the board outside his tavern he had inscribed the following verses of his own composition:—

"Customers came, and I did trust 'em.
So I lost money, and also custom.
To lose them both did vex me sore.
So I resolved to trust no more.
Chalk may be used to any amount.
But chalk won't pay the malt account.

I'm determined to keep a first-rate tap
For ready money, but no strap.
Good-will to all is here intended
Thus, hoping none will be offended.
I remain, yours respectfully
One who's no fool.
i.e. Thomas Hoole."

"What's the meaning of this, Crier Edmed?" asked the landlord.

"Well," answered the bellman, rubbing his nose with the handle of the bell and holding the same by the clapper, "I can't say exactly. My instructions don't go so far. But I fancy the gentlefolk want a spree, and Cornelius Rea at the inn is going to marry again, and wants be rid of his daughter first. It's an ockard affair altogether, and not altogether what it ort to be; and so it has been settled as a mutual accommodation that there shall be a bowling match on the green—and she's to go to the winner. That 's about it. O yes! O yes! O yes!"

Then the crier went forward clanging his bell, and as he progressed more faces appeared at windows and figures at doors, and children swarmed thicker in the street.

Phalanxes of boys formed before and behind, yelling.

"O yes! O yes! O yes! Stewponey Bla is for sale to the highest bidder. Who'll stand another 'apenny and have her? Going, going for tuppence three farthings."

Every now and again the crier made a rush at the boys in front, or backed on those behind, and dispersed them momentarily with the handle of his bell, or with a kick of his foot, and shouted.

"You vagabonds, you! I gave notice of no such thing. How can folk attend to I and learn the truth when you're a hollerin' and a scritchin' them lies! I said she was to be bowled for, and not put up to auction."

"Wot's the difference?" asked an impudent boy.

"One's respectable, 'tother ain't," retorted the crier, who then vigorously swung the bell, and shouted, "O yes! O yes! O yes!" whereat the boys mockingly shouted, "O no! O no! O no!"

A woman who had been kneading bread, with her sleeves turned up and her arms white with flour, crossed the street, came up to the landlord of the New Inn, and accosted him:

"Wot's the meaning of this, I'd like to know?"

"The meaning is before your nose," answered Hoole.

"Where?" inquired the woman, applying her hand at once to the organ, and leaving on it a patch of white.

"I mean," explained the landlord, "that anyone as knows Cornelius Rea knows just about what this signifies."

"I know Cornelius for the matter of that," said the woman from the kneading trough. "Drat my nose, there's sum'ut on it."

"'Tis pollen on your stamen, fair flower," said Hoole. "And if you'll not take it amiss I'll just wipe your nose wi' my apron, and have it off in a jiffy, and an honour it will be to the apron."

"Oh, Mister Hoole, you 're such a flatterer!" said the woman, fresh, stout, matronly; then, "But for all—I don't understand."

"But I do," said the host. "Cornelius is going to be married to that woman—you know whom I mean," with a contemptuous shrug of the shoulder and a curl of the lip.

"I don't know as it's wuss than the goings-on as has been."

"But she's not been in the house; and he can't bring her in till he has got Bladys out."

"But to put her up to be bowled for!"

"That's the doings of the gentlemen—a parcel of bucks and good-for-noughts that frequent the tavern. He's not the man to say them nay. He dussn't go contrary to them—they spend a lot o' money there."

"But who will go in for her?"

"Nay, that's more than I can say. She's a wonderful handsome girl."

"Can't see it," answered the woman.

"No—I always say that for good-looking faces you might go through the three counties and not see one like your own. But, Mrs Fiddian, you're spoiled by looking at your own charms in the glass—it incapacitates you for seeing moderate beauty in another."

"Go along, Mr Hoole."

"How can I go along, when I am opposite you?"

"Come, ha' done with this nonsense. Who are they that have taken a fancy to this white-faced mawken?"

"For one, there is Crispin Ravenhill."

"He can't take her—hasn't enough money."

"He has his barge."

"Wot's that? His uncle would have a word to say about that, I calculate. Who else?"

"There is a stranger staying at the Stewponey that they call Luke Francis."

"What is his trade?"

"Don't know."

"Any others."

"There's Captain Stracey."

"He can't marry her—he's a gentleman; and what about Nan—has he broke with her? What others?"

"Nibblers, only."

"Well, Mr Hoole, I must back to my bakery."

"And I sink back to darkness out of light."

Kinver village occupies a basin in the side of the great rocky ridge that runs for many miles through the country and ends abruptly at the edge, a bluff of sandstone crowned by earthworks, where, as tradition says, King Wulfhere of Mercia had his camp. So far is sure, that the church of Kinver is dedicated to his murdered sons, Wulfhad and Ruffinus. The place of their martyrdom was at Stone, in Staffordshire; but it is possible that their bodies were removed to Kinver.

As already said, the hamlet of Kinver consists mainly of one long street, composed largely of inns, for a highway passes through it; but also of habitations on the slope of the basin.

When the crier had reached the end of the street, he proceeded to ascend a shoulder of hill till he reached a strip of deep red in the sandstone, the colour of clotted blood. Here, according to tradition, a woman was murdered by the Danes, who had ascended the Stour and ravaged Shropshire. From the day of the crime the rock has been dyed blood-red.

At this point the town crier paused and looked about him. The impudent and aggravating boys fell back and pursued him no farther. A sudden awe and dread of consequences came on them, and they desisted from further annoyance. The reason for this will presently transpire.

Kinver parish occupies a peculiar position—it adjoins Shropshire and Worcestershire, and is, in fact, wedged in between the main bulk of Shropshire and an outlying islet in which is Halesowen. It is as though the three counties had clashed at this point, and had resolved their edges into broken fragments, tossed about with little regard to their position.

Kinver takes its name from the Great Ridge, Cefn vawr, of sandstone rock, 542 feet high, that rises as a ness above the plain of the Stour. In that remote period, when the Severn straits divided Wales from England, and the salt deposits were laid that supply brine at Droitwich and in the Weaver Valley, then Kinver Edge stood up as a fine bluff above the ruffling sea. At that time also, a singular insulated sandstone rock that projects upwards as an immense tooth near the roots of the headland stood detached in the water, amidst a wreath of foam, and was haunted by seagulls, and its head whitened with their deposits, whilst its crannies served as nesting-places.

This isolated rock of red sandstone, on and about which Scotch firs have rooted themselves by the name of Holy Austin Rock; but whether at any time it harboured an anchorite of the name of Augustine is a point on which history and tradition are alike silent.

Towards this rock the bellman made his way.

Why so?

Was it for the purpose of summoning jackdaws to the bowling match?

Was it that he desired to hear the echoes answer him from the crag?

We shall see presently.

Although the local tradition is silent relative to a saintly denizen of the rock, it is vocal relative to a tenancy of a different kind. Once it was occupied by a giant and his wife, who with their nails had scooped for themselves caves in the sandstone. The giantess was comely. So thought another giant who lived at Enville.

Now in this sandstone district water is scarce, and the giant of Austin Rock was wont daily to cross a shoulder of hill to a spring some two hundred and fifty yards south of the Rock to fetch the water required for his kitchen. The water oozed forth in a dribble, and the amount required was considerable, for a giant's sup is a drunkard's draught. Consequently he was some time absent. The Enville giant took advantage of this absence to visit his wife. One, two, three. He strode across country, popped his head in, kissed the lady, and retired before her husband returned with the pitchers.

But one day he tarried a moment too long, and the Austin giant saw him. Filled with jealous rage, he set down the pitchers, rushed to the summit of the rock, and hurled a large block at the retreating neighbour. The stone missed its aim; it fell and planted itself upright, and for many generations bore the name of the Bolt Stone. In 1848 the farmer in whose field it stood blew it to pieces with gunpowder.

Mr Edmed, the crier, having reached the foot of Holy Austin Rock, rang a peal and looked up. Instantly the rock was alive. As from a Stilton cheese that is over-ripe the maggots tumble out, so from numerous holes in the cliff emerged women and children. But on the ledge nearest the summit they clustered the thickest.

When the crier saw that he had collected an audience, and that it was attentive, he rang a second peal, and called,—

"O yes! O yes! This is to give notice that this 'ere evening at six o'clock at the Stewponey, there is to be a grand champion match at bowls on the bowling-green. An the prize is to be Bladys Rea, commonly known as Stewponey Bla. Admittance one shilling. 'Arf-a-crown reserved seats, and them tickets admit the bearer to the 'oly function, by kind permission of the proprietor, in the Chapel of Stourton Castle. No 'arf-price. Children and dogs not admitted."

There were three stages of habitations on the rock. From out of the topmost, behind the children, emerged a singular figure—that of an old man in a long snuff-coloured coat, with drab breeches and blue worsted stockings. A white cravat encircled his neck. In his hand he carried a stick. This old man now began to descend the rock with agility such as might not have been anticipated in one of his age.

"Here comes Holy Austin," whispered some boys who had followed the crier at a distance. "Oh my! must we not be good, or we shall get whacks."

The man who approached was not called Austin at his baptism, nor was Austin his surname; nor was the rock called after him, but rather he after the rock; for, having come to inhabit one of the dwellings excavated out of it, in which he kept a day school, the name that had attached to the prong of sandstone adhered to him.

He was more than schoolmaster. He was knobbler at the Church of Kinver—that is to say, it was his office to walk about during divine service, and tap on the head any man or boy overtaken with sleep. The wand of office was painted white, and had a blue knob at the end.

It may now be understood why the boys who had mimicked and surrounded the bellman in the streets of Kinver kept distance and maintained a sober demeanour. Before them was a man who was a schoolmaster, and gave whacks during the week, and who was a knobbler, and could crack their heads on the Sunday. In his double capacity he was a man greatly to be respected and avoided by boys.

To a boy a soldier or a sailor is a joy; a policeman is an object of derision; a ghost is viewed with scepticism; a devil is hardly considered at all; but a schoolmaster is looked on, preferentially from afar, as a concentration of all horrors, and when accentuated with investiture with knobbledom, as something the quintessence of awfulness.

"Repeat again. I didn't hear exactly," said Holy Austin.

The crier obeyed.

The old man lifted up his hands.

"We live in evil days, and I sore fear in an evil place, and the salt that should have seasoned us has lost its savour. There have been no banns called. There can have been no license obtained, seeing none knows who will have the maiden."

"They say the chapel at Stourton is a peculiar," observed the bellman.

The old man shook his head. "This is the beginning of a bad story," said he, and sighed. "Whither will it lead? How and where will it end?"

CHAPTER II. — IN THE CELLAR

The highways from Stafford and Wolverhampton to Kidderminster and the South, and that from Halesowen to Bridgenorth, cross each other at Kinver, and a bridge traverses the Stour, near Stourton Castle, once a royal residence, and one that was a favourite with King John. The great Irish Road from

Bath and Bristol to Chester passed through Kinver, to the great emolument of the town and neighbourhood. At that time, Chester and its port, Park Gate, received the packets from Ireland.

An old soldier in the wars of Queen Anne, a native of the place, settled there when her wars were over, and, as was customary with old soldiers, set up an inn near the bridge, at the cross roads. He had been quartered at Estepona, in the south of Spain, and thence he had brought a Spanish wife. Partly in honour of her, chiefly in reminiscence of his old military days, he entitled his inn, "The Estepona Tavern." The Spanish name in English mouths became rapidly transformed into Stewponey. The spot was happily selected, and as the landlord had a managing wife, and provided excellent Spanish wine, which he imported himself, and with which he could supply the cellars of the gentry round, the inn grew in favour, and established its reputation as one of the best inns in Staffordshire.

The present landlord, Cornelius Rea, was a direct descendant of the founder of the house.

The Stewponey was resorted to by the gentry of the south of Staffordshire, Worcestershire, and Shropshire, on the approach of an election, to decide on the candidates to be proposed and elected.

It was also frequented by travellers on their way north, south, east, or west, who arrived at Kinver at ebb of day, and were disinclined to risk their persons and their purses by proceeding at night over the heaths of Kinver, through the forest of Stourton, and among the broken ground that was held to be a lurking-place for footpads and highway robbers.

Indeed, the neighbourhood for a century bore an evil name, and not without cause. Several and special facilities were here afforded to such as found profit and pleasure in preying on their fellow-men. As already intimated, at this point on the map of England, the territories appertaining to the counties that meet have gone through extraordinary dislocations. There are no natural boundaries, and those which are artificial are capricious. Nothing was more easy for one who desired to throw out his pursuers, armed with a warrant signed by the magistrate of one county, than to pass into the next, and if further pursued by legal process there, to step into a third.

A highwayman, at the beginning of the century in which we live, who honoured Kinver with residing in it, planted his habitation at the extreme verge of the county, divided from the next by a hollow way, and when the officers came to take him, he leaped the dyke, and mocked them with impunity from the farther side.

But this was not all. The geological structure of the country favoured them. Wherever a cliff, great or small, presented its escarpment, there the soft sandstone was scooped out into labyrinths of chambers, in which families dwelt, who in not a few instances were in league with the land pirates. The plunder could anywhere be safely and easily concealed, and the plunderers could pass through subterranean passages out of one county into another, and so elude pursuit.

The highwaymen belonged by no means to the lowest class. The gentlemen of the road comprised, for the most part, wastrels and gamesters of good blood, who thought it no dishonour to recover on the high-road what they had lost on the green table. Occasionally, but only occasionally, one was captured and hung, but the gang was not broken up, the gap was at once refilled. Of applicants there no lack, and the roads remained as insecure before. The facilities for escape at the confines of three counties, and in a country honeycombed with places of refuge, were too many, and the business was too profitable, to enable the sheriffs, during an entire century, to put an end to a condition of affairs which was at once a scandal and a nuisance.

The great canal planned and carried out by Telford runs from the Stour at Stewponey, and passes under a low bluff that is dug out into houses still in occupation. This canal follows the river Stour and connects the Severn, where navigable, with the Grand Trunk Canal, that links the Mersey with the Trent, and connects the St George's Channel with the German Ocean. At the Stewponey, it is joined by the Stourbridge canal. This point is accordingly a centre about which much water traffic gathers, and did gather to a far larger extent before the railroads carried away the bulk of the trade from the canals.

Cornelius Rea, landlord of the Stewponey Inn, was in his cellar, tapping a cask of ale.

He was a stout man, coarse in feature, yet handsome, with one of those vast paunches which caricaturists represent as not uncommon a century ago, but which we never encounter at present. We might suppose that these caricatures were extravagant had we not here and there preserved, as bequests from the past, mahogany dining-tables, with semi-circles cut out of them for the accommodation of the stomachs of stout diners.

The face of Cornelius was red and puffed. It looked peculiarly so, as he stooped at the spigot, by the light of a lamp held by his daughter Bladys. He was in his shirt sleeves, and wore a white nightcap on his head, a yellow, long-flapped waistcoat, and black, shabby knee-breeches.

Bladys was tall and slender—an unusual feature in the district, where women are thickset and short; she had inherited from her Spanish great-grandmother a pale face and dark hair and eyes. She held the light with a trembling hand, not above her head, lest she should set fire to the drapery of cobwebs that hung from the vault. What little daylight penetrated to the cellar fell from the entrance door, and lay pale on the steps that led down into it, in gradually reduced brilliancy, and left the rest of the cellar wholly unillumined.

"It's well up—prime!" said the host. "Fine October brew, this. One cask will never suffice 'em. I'll e'en tap another. Bush-sh-sh! It spits out like an angry cat. It smells good."

He heaved up his clumsy person.

"This stooping don't suit me at my time o' life, girl. What! has the ale spurted into and washed your face?"

"No, father."

"I say it has. Don't contradict me. Your cheeks are wet. I see them glitter. Why dost say 'No, father,' when I say Yes?"

Then all at once a sob broke from her heart.

The heavy man turned his red face and looked at his child. Instinctively she lowered the light.

"Hold up the lamp that I may see!"

She obeyed, but let her head sink on her bosom.

With an oath—he seasoned his every sentence with one—he thrust his hand under her chin, and forced her to raise her face.

"Turn your cheek, wench! What's the sense of this, eh?"

"O father! you put me to shame."

"I—by Ginger! How so?"

"By this bowling match, that is hateful to me—a dishonour; I am ashamed to be seen—and then to send round the crier!"

"Pshaw! Some wenches don't know when they are well off."

"Father! you disgrace me in all men's eyes,—on all lips."

"I! never a bit. It's an honour to any woman to be bowled for. 'Taint every wench can boast she's been an object of contest. My grandmother used to say that in Spain swords were often crossed before a woman could be wed, and that a lady never deemed herself properly married till blood had flowed on her account. Now folk will pay their shillings and half-crowns to see which is the best man. Bless you! There came round a caravan with a giraffe and a laughing hyena, and a roaring lion. Hundreds of people paid sixpence to see these beasts all the way from Africa. Just you think of that. A roaring lion, the king of beasts, only sixpence, let alone the giraffe and the hyena: and shilling and half-a-crown to see you. There's honour and glory, if you like it. I didn't think I'd have lived to see the day and feel such a father's pride, but I do—and I bless you for it. I bet you a spade guinea we shall take the money up in shovels."

"I do not wish it, father."

"I don't care a hanged highwayman whether you wish or not. It is as I choose. Who is the proper person to care and provide for his child but the father? I'm not going to be put off for any foolish girl's whimsies. All the take—every stiver—shall go to you as your portion. I have none other to make."

"I do not desire at all to be married."

"Here you cannot stay. You understand well that you and she as is to be your stepmother can't agree. As soon as you have cleared out, then in comes she; and as I powerfully want her in the house, the sooner you go the better. If you'd taken to her in a friendly and daughterly way, that would have been another matter; but as you have fixed your mind so dead against her there's no help for it. Go you must, and that to-night. And what is more, as a virtuous and respectable man, and a man with a conscience in my stomach, you shall go out respectably, and not be cut off with a shilling. None shall say that of me. I'm a man as does his duty in that station of life and situation as I finds myself in."

"I don't consider it respectable to be bowled for."

"Then I do. I am nigh on forty years older than you, and know the world. Which is most like to be right, you or I? If you leave my house, you leave it respectable."

"If you would suffer me to be alone, I would do nothing that is not respectable."

"Whither would you go? Who would take charge of you? In good sooth, until I put you into the arms of a husband I have no freedom, and unless I do that I am responsible."

Bladys set the lamp on the floor, sank on an empty barrel-horse, covered her face with her hands, and sobbed. The host uttered an oath.

"This angers me. Folly always doth that," said he. "I leave you to yourself whilst I go fetch another spigot, and if you're not in a proper frame of mind when I come back I'll wash your face with stale beer."

The taverner staggered away.

His daughter looked after him as he stumbled up the stair. Then she was left alone in the cellar. The lamp on the floor flickered uneasily in the descending current of air, and the folds of cobwebs waved, catching the light, then disappearing again. The air was impregnated with a savour of mildew and wine and ale. The floor was moist. Spilt liquor had been trodden over the tiles and left them wet and slimy.

Bladys had not been long an orphan. Her mother had died but a few months ago, after a lengthy and painful illness. She had been a shrewd, firm woman, an excellent manageress, who had kept order in the house and controlled her husband. Cornelius was a weak, vain man, and he allowed himself to be swayed by his customers, especially by those of the best class.

During the protracted illness of his wife he had shown attention to a woman of indifferent character, showy in dress, whom he had introduced into the inn to relieve his wife of her duties. This had caused painful scenes, much recrimination, and the sick woman had with difficulty persuaded her husband to send the woman away. Her last hours had been embittered by the thought that her child might have this worthless creature as her stepmother, and by the vexation of knowing that the fruits of her care, saving, and labour would go to enrich this person, whom she despised, yet hated.

Hardly was his wife dead before Cornelius showed plainly what were his intentions. It became a matter of jest at his table, of scandal in the village.

In talking with some of the gentle bucks and topers who frequented his house, Cornelius had had the indiscretion to comment on the difficulty he felt in disposing of his daughter before introducing his new wife to Stewponey; and the suggestion had been made in jest that he should have her bowled for, and give as her dower the money made on the occasion. He accepted the suggestion gravely, and then several chimed in to press him to carry it into execution.

Associating as Cornelius did with men coarse-minded and, whatever their social position, of no natural refinement, casting aside, when at his table, or about his fire, whatever polish they had, Rea was in no way superior to his companions. He was incapable of understanding what belonged to his duty as a father, and of treating with the delicacy due to her sex and situation the solitary girl who was dependent on him.

Bladys loved her father, without respecting him.

He would not allow his guests to address her in an unseemly manner, but his protection extended no further.

The girl was fully aware that she could not remain in the Stewponey after her father was married again. To do so, she must forfeit her self-respect and do a wrong to the memory of her mother.

The girl's pale and stately beauty of foreign cast had brought many admirers about her. Amongst others she had been subjected to the addresses of a certain Captain George Stracey, who occupied a small house in the parish, was in good society, and seemed possessed of means. But both she and her father were well aware that his addresses were not honourable. She had repelled him with icy frigidity, that was but an intensification of her ordinary demeanour to the guests.

Another who had been forward in his endeavours to win her regard was a man then lodging at the inn, who had been there a fortnight, and gave Luke Francis as his name. His home, he intimated, was at Shrewsbury, his profession something connected with the law. He was a fine man, with broad shoulders, a firm mouth, and high cheek-bones.

There was a third admirer, Crispin Ravenhill, a bargeman, owning his own boat on the canal. But although his admiration might be gathered from his deep earnest eyes, he never addressed a word to the girl to intimate it. He was a reserved man of nearly thirty, who associated with few of his fellows. It was held that the influence of his uncle, Holy Austin, who had reared him from boyhood, still surrounded him and restrained him from those vices which were lightly esteemed in that age and by the class of men to which he pertained.

There was yet another, Lewis Falcon, a young man of private means sufficient to free him from the obligation of working for his livelihood, and who spent his substance in drink, gambling, and dog-fighting.

Bladys looked at the cobwebs. Never had she seen a fly in the cellar, yet here they hung, dense, long, ghostly. And she—was not she enveloped in cobwebs? Whither could she escape? In what direction look? Where see light? She remained with her head between her hands till hope, expectation of release, died in her heart; her tears dried up; her agitation ceased. She had become as stone in her despair.

CHAPTER III. — CRISPIN

"Bla! run, take a jug of ale to Ravenhill," called the host down the cellar stairs. "He's come for his luncheon."

Bladys hastily wiped her eyes and mounted the steps, fetched what was required, and went into the guest-room, where Crispin, the bargeman, was pacing.

"I will not have it here. Outside," said he, "under the elm." And then went forth.

The girl followed.

Crispin Ravenhill was a tall man, with fair hair, yet were his eyes dark; they were large, velvety; and a gentle, iridescent light played, passing in waves through them. Unlike the men of his time, he was completely unshaven, and wore a long light beard and moustache.

He seated himself on a bench beneath one of those "Worcester weeds," as the small-leaf elm is termed; and as Bladys placed his bread and cheese on a table there, he looked attentively at her.

"You have been weeping," said he.

"I have cause, when about to be thrust from my home," she answered, in a muffled voice. She resented his remark, yet was unable to restrain an expression of the bitterness that worked within.

"And with whom will you leave home?" he asked.

"That the bowls decide, not I."

Then she turned to leave; but he caught her wrist. "You shall not go. Much depends on what now passes between us," said he.

"What passes between us is bread and cheese from me to thee, and seven-pence in return."

"If that be all, go your way," said he. "Yet no; you have tears in your heart as well as in your eyes. Sit down and let us speak familiarly together."

"I cannot sit down," answered she—for indeed it would have been indecorous for her to seat herself along with a customer. She might converse with him standing for half-an-hour with impunity, but to sit for one minute would compromise her character. Such was tavern etiquette.

"I pity you, my poor child, from the deep of my heart; in very deed I am full of pity."

There was a vibration in his rich, deep voice, a flutter of kindly light in his brown eyes that sent a thrill through the heart of Bladys. In a moment her eyes brimmed, and he was conscious of a quiver in the muscles of the wrist he grasped.

"They make sport of you. 'Give not that which is holy unto dogs, neither cast ye your pearls before swine,' was not spoken of lifeless objects, but of living jewels, of consecrated beings. They make sport of you to your shame, and to that of the entire place. But the place can take of itself—not so thou, poor child."

She did not speak.

"God help you," he continued. "A frail, white lily planted, springing out of a good soil,—and to be plucked up by the roots and transplanted, none can say whither."

Never hitherto had any one spoken to Bladys in this manner. There was something pedantic in his mode of speech, formed by contact with his uncle; but there was genuine sincerity in the tone of voice, real sympathy breaking out in flashes from his opalescent eyes.

The mother of Bladys had been a good but a hard woman, practical not imaginative, kind but unsympathetic; engrossed in her own grievances, she had been incapable of entering into the soul of her child, and showing motherly feeling for its inarticulate yearnings and vague shrinkings.

"This is none of your doing," proceeded Crispin. "To this you gave no consent."

Her lips moved. She could not speak.

"Nay," said he, "I need no words."

There was a mellowness, a gentleness in his tone and mode of speech that won the confidence of the girl. Hitherto he had not spoken to her except on ordinary matters, and she had seen nothing of his heart. In Nature, all is harmonious—the flower and its leaf are in one key. In a landscape are no jarring contrasts. It is so in human beings; look and voice and manner correspond with the inner nature; they are, in fact, its true expression. The stern and unsympathetic heart has its outward manifestations,—the harsh voice and the hard eye, and severity of line in figure and feature. The gross soul has an unctuous look, a sensual mouth, and a greasy voice. But the pitiful and sweet soul floods every channel of utterance with its waters of love. The kindly thought softens and lights up the eye, and gives to the vocal chords a wondrous vibration. However lacking in beauty and regularity the features may be, however shapeless the form, the inner charity transfigures all into a beauty that is felt rather than seen. "There is no fear in love," said the Apostle; the saying may be supplemented with this—neither is there ugliness where is Charity.

And now this solitary girl, solitary in the midst of turmoil, was for the first time in her life aware that she was in the presence of one who could understand her troubles, and who stretched forth to help her and sustain her in her recoil from the false position into which she had been thrust.

As Bladys declined to take a seat, Crispin stood up. He did not release her wrist. She made an effort to disengage herself, but it was not sincere, nor was it persistent, and he retained hold.

"Nay," said he, "I will not suffer you to escape till you have answered my questions. This may be the last time I ever have a word with you; consider that; and I must use the moment You stand at a turning-point in your life, and even so do I. Answer me, in the first place, how came this mad affair about?"

She hesitated and looked down

"Speak openly. Tell me everything about it."

"There is little to relate."

"Then relate that little."

"It is this. My father is about to marry again."

"I have heard as much."

"To Catherine Barry, and I must leave the house."

"Catherine!" said Crispin. "That name is given as my uncle would say as lucus a non lucendo, and as mons a non movendo. Excuse my speaking words of Latin. It comes to me from my schoolmaster and all-but father. I understand that you must leave. It cannot be other. Catherine Barry and you cannot be under one roof."

"And one evening when the gentlemen were at Stewponey drinking—then something my father said about it, and added that he supposed he must have me married, and so rid the house of me. But to do that he lacked money, as none would have a portionless girl."

"There he spake false."

"And then," proceeded Bladys, "the gentlemen being in drink, and ready for any frolic, swore there should be sweepstakes for me. They would each give something, and make the beginning of the fund, and my father should announce a game of bowls, each candidate for the prize to pay a guinea, and the whole to go to me and the winner. Then they sent a punch-bowl round the table, and some put in five and some three, and one even ten guineas, and so started the fund with forty-six guineas. After that my father considered he could not go back."

"And so sacrifices his child," said the young boatman between his teeth.

"My father is calling me," said Bladys hastily.

"I let you go on one condition only—that you return; and you shall return with an answer. Bla, if you will take me, say so. I am a poor man, with my boat only; but with God's help I will maintain you with honour. Take me, and I will snatch you away before this hideous scandal can take place, and you become the talk of the country."

Again the voice of the landlord called.

"I must run," said Bladys, changing colour.

"Then go, and return with an answer, Yes or No."

She left.

Whilst away, Crispin Ravenhill stood motionless, leaning against the table, with his arms folded and his dark eyes fixed on the ground. His contracted fingers alone showed that he was a prey to disturbing thoughts.

As he thus stood, a strong dark man came up, and brushed rudely against him. Crispin glanced at him with an expression of annoyance, and recognised the stranger, Luke Francis.

"You have much to say to that wench," said the latter.

"Whether I have or no concerns you not. Go your way, and for the future, when you pass a man, measure your distance more nicely."

"I shall go where I list, and those that stand in my way I shall thrust out of it."

"Those who jar against others must expect bruises."

Ravenhill threw his weight on the end of the table so as to tilt up the opposite end, and he then swung it round against the elbow of Francis, which it struck. The man thus hit sprang up with an exclamation of pain, and clapped his hand to the joint for a moment. Francis did not speak for a minute, but after that he flared out in rage—

"So you will try issue with me?"

"I have no further quarrel with you. You, having rudely thrust against me, have received a thrust in return. Our account is balanced."

"You are not afraid to provoke me?"

"Not in the smallest degree."

"Look at my arms."

Francis extended his hands, and then, indeed, Ravenhill observed how long the arms were; unduly so, out of proportion to his lower limbs; for when he lowered his hands they touched his knees. The stranger now bent his arms, and the muscles swelled like knotted cables. Then he laughed.

"There are few like me. I could take your head between my palms, and squeeze it as you would a Seville orange. Are you one that has entered for the bowling match?"

"I am not."

"I am sorry for that, for I would like to be pitted against you. Perhaps you will not deny me a cast at wrestling; that will give more spirit than a game at bowls."

Before Ravenhill was ready with an answer, the inn-keeper arrived, with Bladys following him.

"What is this?" he asked. "You, Crispin, stepping in and trying to forestall everyone? That's against all laws of gaming. Look here, Mr Francis. This boatman has been asking my wench to let him carry her off afore the match. That's unfair dealing all the world over. I say it can't be."

"And it shan't," said Luke Francis.

"It can't and it shan't," shouted the host. "Why, there's forty-six guineas paid down by the gentlemen, as'd be all forfeited without the match. They gave it on condition; and I reckon that we shall have a take nigh on twenty pounds, what with the gate and with the sale of liquor and the stakes. It'd be a flying in the face of Fortune. Besides which it'd not be honourable; and I pride myself—I haven't got so much to pride myself on, but I do on that—as I'm a straight, honourable man in all my dealings."

"I have paid my guinea. I demand my right to contest for the prize—and win—to take her off," said the stranger.

"And he—has he staked?" asked the host.

"No, he has not," retorted Francis. "He told me so himself."

"I have had the crier round the neighbourhood. All the world will be here. Am I to befool them? It cannot be."

Then Ravenhill stood forth.

"I have sought to save the poor girl from a cruel and wanton insult, your house of Stewponey from the acquisition of a bad name, our vicar from the commission of an act which he will repent in his sober moments, and the parish from a scandal."

"And I refuse your interference," said Cornelius.

"What does she decide?" asked the barge-man. But Bladys was too frightened to reply.

"I answer for her. I am responsible. If you want her," said the taverner, "put down your guinea like a man, and try your chance with the rest. We'll have no underhand dealings here."

"Stewponey Bla," said Crispin, "is it your desire that I should enter for you?"

She nodded. She could not speak.

"Then here is my guinea."

He cast the coin on the table.

"May God give her to me!" he added with suppressed emotion. "Would I could have won her any way but this."

CHAPTER IV. — THE BOWLING-GREEN

THE ancient bowling-green at the Stewponey remains in good condition to the present day, although the once popular and excellent English pastime of bowls has there, as elsewhere, fallen into desuetude.

In old England there was not a village, country house, without its bowling-green. A century ago the game held its own steadily, and it is within the last seventy or eighty years only that it has lost favour and has been supplanted by croquet and lawn tennis.

A bowling-green was necessarily sixty yards in length and half that in breadth, so that the space required was considerable. The rustic bowler on the village green had to make allowance for the inequalities of the ground, but the gentleman player used every precaution that his green should be absolutely even, the grass unbroken by groundsel and daisy, and smooth and short as velvet pile.

The bowling ground at the Stewponey, hedged about with small-leafed elms, well elevated above the road and river, and consequently dry, constituted a prime attraction to the inn, and the landlord spared no pains to keep it in order. The sward might compare with that in any nobleman's grounds. The bowls with which the game was played were not precisely the same as those now manufactured. They had the shape of flattened oranges, and were loaded with lead inserted in one side to serve as bias, or tendency wards the end of the course to describe a sweep. When delivered, the ball runs directly to its end, but as soon as it reaches the point where the force that launched it is expended, then it curls, carried by the weight of the lead, and turns in an arc. And it is here, in the practical knowledge of the effect of the bias, that the difficulty of the game consists, and the skill of the player is exhibited.

Nor is this all. At the present day, all bowls are of a standard size and regulation weight. But formerly it was not so. The bowls were turned by the village carpenter, and little nicety was observed as to the amount of lead inserted. Those on the village green, those on the Squire's lawn, those on the alehouse ground, were not of necessity of the same weight and size. Not only so, but among the bowls on the same green there existed no exact uniformity. The bowls were numbered in pairs, and the players either drew for their numbers, or, if accustomed to meet for the game on the same turf, adhered to their numbers, and so acquired perfect familiarity with the peculiarities of their several bowls. When no game could be played with zest except for money, whether cards, bowls, or pulling straws, there was ever a risk of fraud; and to this the game under consideration lent itself with peculiar facility, as it was an easy matter to tamper with the bias, and so alter the character of the run of the ball.

Cornelius Rea was not disappointed in his anticipation that the advertisement of the match would draw the entire neighbourhood together at his inn. Indeed, all the neighbouring parishes had decanted their male population into the grounds of the Stewponey, whilst the road without was choked with women and children, and such men as could not afford to pay for admission. Boys had climbed trees, girls were thrusting their heads through gaps in thorn hedges, in hopes of obtaining a view free of cost.

Will anyone say that what is here described is and was impossible? That it is impossible at the close of the nineteenth century may be at once admitted, but it was quite otherwise with the latter half of the century that is gone. It is hard, almost impossible, for us to conceive that things were witnessed by our grandfathers which seem to us quite incredible. To disarm criticism, then, let me affirm that just such a contest for a woman, as is here described, did take place, and in the very same parish of Kinver, so late as within the first twenty years of the century which our readers render illustrious by living in it. On this occasion the woman entertained a decided and tender preference for one of the competitors, and unhappily he proved unsuccessful. Nevertheless, she loyally adhered to the compact entered into before the game was played, and married the man who was victor, and for whom she entertained no liking. An united and happy couple they proved to be.

To their credit be it mentioned that no women entered the wicket of the Stewponey; not that they were less interested in the contest than the men, but that they were restrained by a sense of decorum. Nevertheless, as already intimated, they congregated in the road in such dense masses as to impede traffic, and run the risk of being thrown down by the horses of some of the sporting squires who rode up or drove in their buggies to see the unusual fun of a woman being bowled for.

If they were debarred witnessing the game, they would have the gratification of seeing the prize carried off to Stourton Chapel, there to be married. If the women held back under some restraint, this was not the case with certain men who should have been leaders of the people—the parson, the doctor, and two magistrates. Of gentlemen there were over a score, of parsons happily only one, but he—the vicar of the parish.

The vicar of Kinver at this time was the Reverend Timothy Toogood—red-faced, rheumy-eyed, dressed in the shabbiest clerical garb.

The vicar was miserably poor. He was overshadowed by the evening lecturer, who received double the income of the other, without having any further responsibility laid on him than to preach one sermon on Sunday. Vicar and lecturer lived in perpetual feud, and, it must be allowed, the former laid himself open to reproach by his indiscretions and irregularities. The living hardly merited the name. It was more deserving to be reckoned as a dying. The vicarage was a mean cottage. The parishioners might have made their parson's position tolerable, and have secured a respectable incumbent, had they consented to give the lectureship to the vicar, but the latter was a nominee of the Leathersellers' Company, and the villagers delighted to exhibit their independence by appointing their own lecturer.

The main politics of the place consisted in controversy over the merits or demerits of the two ecclesiastics, and in setting one against the other. It is of no use denying the fact that poverty in certain positions demoralises. A common workman can be poor and straight as a whistle, but a man of some education and parts, and born a gentleman, if in reduced circumstances, is tempted almost beyond power of resistance to deflect from the straight course. Parson Toogood, had he been in comfortable circumstances, would have been respectable and have deserved respect. He was kind-hearted and unselfish. But his distresses deprived him of self-esteem, and blunted his moral perception. He saw one only chance of escape into a position of ease, and that was by becoming the humble servant of the Squire, not daring to oppose him lest he should lose his favour and the chance of promotion to a fat living in his gift.

Some scruple did enter the mind of the vicar when it was announced to him that he was expected to consecrate the union determined by a game of bowls, but the scruple was laid at rest by the insistence of Squire Stourton that unless he performed the sacred rite the couple would go off without it, and he clenched the argument with a promise of five guineas as fee.

Some scruple did enter the mind of the vicar, because it was impossible to publish banns or provide a licence before the contest decided who the man was who was to be united with Stewponey Bla, and no time afterwards was available, as the marriage was to follow immediately on the conclusion of the game. But this scruple yielded under the consideration that the Stourton Castle chapel was a peculiar, not under Episcopal jurisdiction, and that, therefore, as his patron said, "My dear Toogood, you may do in it just what you like; stand on your head if you will, and bless the happy pair with your toes. No one can object."

Seeing that Squire Stourton was a magistrate, the vicar assumed he ought to know the law, an assumption as great and hazardous as one that pre-supposed that every vicar was acquainted with theology. When, moreover, the Squire added, "My dear fellow, if you have any hesitation in the matter, make yourself easy. I will call in the lecturer," then every symptom of hesitation subsided.

"Make way for the umpire!" shouted the host, elbowing the crowd to the right and left. "Parson Toogood is umpire. Room for his reverence!"

The garden was full to overflow with a coarse and noisy throng of men, and the drawers had difficulty in supplying them with ale, so closely were they packed and so thirsty were the constituent atoms. As if to intimate to Bladys that retreat was impossible, the woman Catherine Barry had been called in to direct and control the house for that day. The host could not manage everything. Bladys was incapacitated by the part she had to play. Assistance he was obliged to invoke. What more reasonable than that he should summon her who was shortly to become mistress in the house? But for all that, her presence was an outrage—so the unhappy girl felt it.

The gentlemen who had paid their half-crowns occupied benches on three sides of the bowling-green. Those who had paid but a shilling stood behind them and in rear of the "footer," whence the players cast the bowls.

"Come up to the head," shouted one fellow to his mate. "I want to get a good sight of Stewponey Bla, and find out from her face which is her fancy man."

"I don't care a hang for her fancy—I want to follow the game."

"Well, you can see it finely from the top."

"Now, Roger," exclaimed another in the crush, "I'll thank you to keep your elbows in. You've spilt my ale. Good luck; it's over your mulberry cloth, and not over my new coat."

"What do you want ale for now?"

"How can I see till I've washed my eyes?"

"How many have paid up their stakes?"

"There's Tup Rivers."

"Tup Rivers! Well, that's comical. But I suppose he's aiming after the fifty or sixty guineas he's heard the gentlefolk have subscribed. I didn't think he was a marrying man."

"Lor' bless y'—any man would marry for fifty pounds."

"Has Lewis staked?"

"Ay ay, but he's too drunk to keep his legs. The Captain paid, but won't play."

"Nan has been at him—that's it."

"That stranger chap—he's in it."

"Who is he?"

"Heaven above can answer better than I. Then they tell me Crispin the bargeman has entered."

At that moment a shout and a groan. The interlocutors pressed up to the head, where sat the umpire, to learn the occasion. Tup Rivers had withdrawn, and was asking to have his guinea returned. He was a small farmer. He shrank from a game in which he would have as his opponents such men as Francis and Ravenhill.

"Then," said the man entitled Roger, "the game has thinned down amazingly to two—that's sorry sport. But for seeing who wins the prize I'd go away. Come, Matthew—a stranger against Kinver, What odds? I'll lay on Kinver, for the honour of the old place."

To revert to the first couple who were in dialogue. "Look," said one, "observe Stewponey Bla; she hangs her head, you can't see her face."

"Pshaw!" answered the man addressed. "What right has a publican's daughter to be shamefaced? It don't belong to the profession—it's put on for the occasion, take my word for it."

"Silence! They have begun."

A hush fell on the spectators. It was as intimated. Two competitors had withdrawn at the last moment, and one was incapacitated. It had been hoped that a sixth would enter before the game began, but none had done so. The number was reduced to two. Precedence in entry entitled to selection of bowls. The choice lay with Francis. Each was to have four. The stranger chose the twos and fours. The odd numbers were left to Crispin.

A hush fell on the spectators as Luke Francis cast the jack and set the mark rightly enough beyond twenty-one yards from the footer. Haying done this, he at once delivered his first bowl, that spun along merrily to the right, slackened its pace as it neared the point of distance required, then halted, turned and ran with a sweep towards the jack and touched it. The ball was so brilliantly delivered and the execution so admirable, that it was greeted with a shout of applause; but a louder shout welcomed Crispin's success, as with a swift ball he struck the bowl of his adversary from its place, and knocked it from the green.

"Dead!" shouted the onlookers.

Francis played again, and this time came wide of the jack. Ravenhill looked steadily at his goal, swung his arm twice and delivered the bowl. It lagged, came to an apparent rest, and then twisted away from the jack. The ball of Francis was not within standard distance, and therefore did not count.

Again Francis delivered, and his bowl made a revolution and rested within a few inches of the jack. Crispin paused, took deliberate measure and made his cast. To his surprise the ball halted, turned over, and rested without further activity. At once he walked the length of the green, to where the balls lay, stooped, took up his bowl, and strode before the umpire.

"Parson Toogood," said he, "look here! Did you ever see a bowl settle with the bias upwards? I demand that this be seen into."

Several of the gentlemen sitting near rose and pressed round, the spectators in the rear jumped the bench and crowded round.

The vicar took the bowl in question, "Fetch me Ravenhill's other," said he, and was at once obeyed.

The vicar weighed one against the other in his hands.

"I confess this one seems the lightest," he said, referring to the bowl that had rested with the lead mark upwards.

"Hand it to the Squire," said Ravenhill, "let him investigate it further."

Mr Stourton took the bowl, and with his pocket-knife removed the plug that closed the opening which usually contained the bias. The lead was gone.

"The bowls are imperfect. There has been an accident to one," said Parson Toogood. "The game must be begun afresh."

"There has been no accident," said Ravenhill. "There has been an attempt to cheat."

"Do you charge me?" asked Luke Francis. "It was not in the interest of any one else to defeat me. You, lodging in the house, had access to the bowls."

Then rose an angry confused shout of "Cheat! cheat! The stranger is caught cheating! To the duckpond with him! Kick him out!"

Francis raised himself to his full height, and in a loud voice thundered, "I am no rogue. It has been a chance. Ravenhill has accused me. I defy him. Let us fight it out. That is better sport than a game at bowls."

This proposition instantly allayed the gathering wrath. Shouts arose of "Ay! ay! Fair play! Fight the matter out!"

But the vicar in much agitation stood up, his red face becoming mottled like soap.

"No!" cried he, "I'll be no party to a fight. A game of bowls is harmless; but a fight—no, I cannot, dare not countenance that. If you will, let them wrestle, but no pugilism. I will allow that."

"Then let us wrestle," said Luke.

The crowd shouted, "We are content, let them wrestle."

"Strip and prepare," said Luke to Crispin.

"I have desired this."

CHAPTER V. — THE JACK

Quickly the two men prepared for the struggle. They threw off their coats and waistcoats, and then proceeded to remove their boots.

Usually a girdle was cast over the right shoulder of each wrestler, and was buckled under the left arm; but this was done only when the shirt was removed. On the present occasion both antagonists and spectators were too impatient to tarry till suitable belts could be procured, and the two men were therefore content to confront each other as they were, the right hand of the one on the left side of the other, and the left hand on his antagonist's right shoulder, looking into each other's eyes, and with ears alert for the signal to begin.

One—two—three!

Then they stood with contracted brows, set lips, swaying from side to side, the muscles rippling under the skin in their exposed limbs. Then, suddenly, they grappled.

From the first round, Crispin ascertained two things. In the first place, his antagonist was comparatively inexperienced; in the next, his boast of superior strength was justified. It was obvious to him that the contest would be one in which in his opponent moderate skill was combined with extraordinary force.

Crispin had not played often; only occasionally had he tried a fall with a comrade, and he had never taken to the sport seriously.

The clutch of Luke Francis's hand on Crispin's shoulder told him that, could his adversary get the other hand in the same position on his other shoulder, Francis would be able to double him backwards and throw him, or snap his spine. But if Luke was the most muscular in arm, Crispin had superior agility, in that his legs were longer than those of his opponent.

After the first round—that proved without result—they desisted, so as to gather breath.

Then they made ready for a second bout.

For a minute, as before, the two opponents stood swaying, otherwise motionless, and then by a sudden and simultaneous impulse, each clasped the other round the waist.

Bladys sat near the head of the bowling-green, too frightened, too bewildered to have eyes to see what went forward, or ears to hear the comments that passed. She sat in a dream, but the dream was a nightmare.

For some days she had been in a condition of nervous excitation, her brain in a whirl. And now she was as one stupefied, unconscious of what passed before, about her.

She had tortured her mind to discover some method to escape from the predicament in which she was placed, and had found none. A hundred years ago, young unmarried women were not the emancipated beings that they are now. At present, a girl who is impatient of the restraints of home, or desires a change from its monotony, can enter a post-office, go behind a counter, or offer to be a cook, and be overwhelmed with applications for her inefficient services. A century ago, the case was wholly different. There were no situations open to women save those that were menial, and such as entered service were either apprenticed for three years, or hired at a statute fair for one. A twelvemonth was then the shortest term of service, whereas now, should a girl dislike her situation, not finding any eligible young men within attraction, she can say, "I will go at the end of a month," and away she flits.

Moreover, a hundred years ago, servants were kept only in the houses of the gentry and in farms. The tradesmen attended to their business, and their wives looked after the house. At that time there was vast competition for a place, whereas now the tables are reversed; there is competition among mistresses for a servant.

And further still, discipline was then drawn tighter, and the children dared not oppose their wishes to the will of their parents; least of all, in such a matter as settlement in life.

What could Bladys do as matters then were? In some instances a girl broke through the net, and eloped. But to elope it takes two; and the offer of Crispin Ravenhill came too late for her to take advantage of it. She had, moreover, no ambition to jump into any man's arms; her sole desire was to escape from the many arms which were extended to receive her.

She had not slept for several nights, nor had she been allowed any repose during the day. Wounded to the quick in her self-respect—and with her Spanish blood Bladys had inherited something of Spanish pride—trembling at the threshold of an unknown future, aching at being thrust from the home of her childhood, offended at the insult offered to the memory of her mother, she had been brought by exhaustion of physical and mental powers to a condition in which all her faculties were at a standstill. Now, at the supreme moment that determined her future, she was as one in a trance, in the very ecstacy of despair. Her face was white, her brow beaded with drops of agony, and her head declining on her bosom. Her hands, folded in her lap, twitched convulsively.

Although she felt the vibration in her feet from the trampling of the antagonists on the sward, yet she alone of all the crowd seemed unconcerned as to the issue of the game. Now and then she raised her head mechanically and looked at the writhing figures, but it was with lack-lustre eyes, and she almost immediately let it fall again.

When the green had been cleared for the wrestling match, the jack had been flung aside and had rested at the feet of Bladys; and in fact it appeared as though she were more intent on trifling with this little ball than in watching the conflict, for she had her toe on it and played the jack forward and backward with it, now letting it run almost beyond reach, then stretching her foot so as to recover it and recommence her play. Had not those who surrounded her had all their attention fixed on the struggling men, they would have observed and commented on her behaviour as one that exhibited extraordinary callousness. Yet callous she was not, only in that stunned mental and moral condition in which only what is infinitely insignificant is perceived, and the faculties are dead to everything of genuine importance.

Already with a thud both men had gone down, and had gone down together; but so uncertain was it which had cast the other that the umpire declared it was a "dog-fall," and that the contest must be recommenced.

A simple and elementary stratagem in wrestling is for the one to work his right shoulder under the armpit of his opponent. By this means he obtains enormous leverage, displaces the centre of gravity of his antagonist, and is able to upset him. Crispin, relying on the inexperience of Luke, attempted this trick, but the stratagem was so obvious that Francis was prepared to resist it.

Before long the wrestling match altered its character, and degenerated into a fight. Ravenhill in vain endeavoured to adhere to the laws of the game, and in vain also did the umpire remonstrate. Francis knew or cared nothing about regulations. All he sought was by all means to master his adversary, and to bring him to the ground.

And although at first the spectators shouted their disapproval of manifest violations of rule, yet when they saw that the blood of both combatants was up, and that they were resolved on something more serious than a wrestling match, they were quite prepared to encourage the new direction taken, for to them the greater the violence employed and the greater the danger to life and limb in those engaged, the more acute was their pleasure, and the more interesting the sport.

If, according to regulation, either party break his hold—that is to say, lets go, whilst the other retains his grip—the one so leaving go is counted the loser; and his letting go is regarded as equivalent to a fall. But to this rule Francis paid no attention.

When he suddenly disengaged his hands and laid hold of Ravenhill by the arm to force them from him, the crowd shouted "Rule! rule!" but as he paid no regard to the call, and the struggle became more intense, they no longer protested, and allowed it to proceed in such manner as suited the opponents, and suffered them to use such devices as they chose for obtaining advantage one over the other.

Every now and then from the spectators rose a burst of applause, like the roar of a wave clashing against a rock. Then ensued a hiss, like the retreat of a wave over a shingly beach, caused by all together drawing in their breath between their teeth.

At one moment the eyes were dazzled by a whirl of limbs, in the midst of which one body was indistinguishable from another. Then followed a pause—a pause in which all was a-quiver. And in that pause Luke was seen with his hands one on each side of the temples of Crispin, endeavouring to work his thumbs to his eye-sockets, so as to force out the balls, or compel his adversary to give way, and let go his hold, so as to save them. Crispin held Luke about the waist, and endeavoured to give him "the click," which consists in drawing the opponent to the chest, so as to force him to resist and drag backward, then to strike his left leg with the right, and if he be pressing back at the moment, he is prevented from recovering his balance, and reels over.

It was whilst attempting this well-known stratagem that Luke disengaged his arms, and was working his thumbs to the eye-sockets of the boatman, only prevented from effecting his purpose by the movement of Ravenhill's head, and by his own uncertain footing.

At this moment, unconscious of what she was about, Bladys pressed the jack with her toe, so as to flip it from her. It shot forward, and ran under the feet of the combatants.

Crispin trod on it at the moment when he trusted to have his antagonist off the ground; instead, he slipped, was upset, fell, bringing Luke down upon him, and, in falling, he came with the back of his head on the jack.

Francis instantly disengaged himself, sprang to his feet, and waved his arms triumphantly. Ravenhill lay prostrate on his back, speechless and unconscious, blood running between his lips. The crowd had not noticed the incident of the jack. What they saw was the fall of Crispin, with Luke above him, and that the stranger was the victor.

In a moment the bowling-green was inundated by men cheering, to get at Francis, slap his back, and shake hands with him.

"Stand back!" shouted the vicar. "You will trample on the fallen man."

"Has he broke his back?"

"Or his head?"

"Never mind him. Come on! Parson, run for your surplice. There'll be a double entertainment. A wedding first and a burying after."

"And a hanging as a finish-up withal, if he has been killed."

"That would be rare sport; but there's no chance of that. It's but accidental homicide. More's the pity."

"I wouldn't ha' missed the sight for a crown."

"On to the chapel!"

Then the landlord bustled up to his daughter. "Bla," said he, panting and swelling, "along with me. Luke Francis is your man. You're in luck's way. The captain never meant aught but mischief, and Lewis is a drunken sot. Hey! Wish you joy, Mr Francis."

The victor, breathless, hot and dishevelled, was reinvesting himself in waistcoat and coat; then he drew on his boots, and adjusted his cravat. He did not trouble himself about the prostrate man. But the village surgeon was there, and he forced the crowd apart whilst he examined him.

"How came the jack here?" he asked.

"The jack was kicked off the field. I did it myself," said a man who stood by.

"The jack is here now, and, in falling on it, Ravenhill has been injured," said the surgeon.

"Ay, I saw it spin over the turf, and he tripped on it," said a second.

"Never heed. This is doctor's business," shouted several.

"Come along! To Stourton chapel! Parson's on the way."

In another minute the bowling-green was deserted, save by the surgeon kneeling over the insensible Crispin.

And the crowd, as it swept like a torrent out of the garden, along the road, carried Stewponey Bla with it.

Half-A-Crown ticket-holders alone admitted. We shilling people remain without. It is as well. The scene in the chapel cannot be edifying, considering who they are that press in, fox-hunting, dog-fighting, cocking, country gentry, some already half-tipsy, Lewis Falcon wholly so; the parson a man of indifferent character; the marriage the result of a fight.

Stourton Castle, once the favourite residence of King John, and possessing a venerable history, built originally of red sandstone, had been given a rakish modern aspect by a proprietor who conceived that what was old must be bad, and whose taste was at the service of the fashion of the day. He had delivered over this ancient structure to an architect to modernise at the period when taste was at the lowest ebb in England.

At one time the Castle had been surrounded by an extensive deer park, in which were stately oaks of the growth of centuries. Card-playing, dicing, toping, law-suits, had reduced the Squires of Stourton to the cutting down of their oaks, and the selling them so as to pay with the proceeds their debts of honour and of dishonour.

The second half of last century was a period when something more than artistic taste had reached its lowest depth. Common morality and the sense of decency were equally depraved. At the close of the seventeenth century, moral corruption had been open and flagrant in high quarters, but a religious leaven was in the land, and there was a sturdy substance and inner core of virtue to be found among the middle and lower classes, an hereditary, traditional respect for what was good and true and honest.

But with the expulsion of the Non-jurors, those who were respectable in life and learning were driven from the pulpits of the Church, and their places were occupied by time-servers, by men of inferior moral, mental, and social position. The relics of Puritanism had been too narrow, too sour to influence the mass of mankind. Dissociating themselves from all amusements, however harmless, condemning them as evil, holding together in small acrid clusters, the Saints had done nothing to check and moderate what was boisterous, and their very extravagance of strictness made of their sons the most debauched and shameless when freed from parental control. The decay which had begun at the head under the last Stuarts worked slowly yet steadily downwards: it attacked the heart of the community, and then sent rottenness to the very roots, in the time of the last Georges.

In few parts of England was there more hard drinking, hard swearing, law-breaking, and licentious living than in that portion of the Midlands where the scene of our tale lies. There, as already intimated, the convergence and dislocation at point of contact of three counties afforded every opportunity for making light of the law.

Often a fat living rewarded a complaisant tutor who would marry the discarded mistress of his patron; as often the best way to preferment in the Church was for the clerk in orders to be a fellow-sot with the man who presented to the cure of souls where spread his acres.

Had Parson Toogood lived near Lichfield, he would have been respectable in conduct, and only forfeited his dignity by cringing and spittle-licking to the Bishop, but as Lichfield was a long way off he toadied his squire.

"Here they come!"

The crowd became agitated, compacted itself closer, broke out into jocosity, and was broad in its mirth, noisy in its ejaculations.

Out through the doorway burst a couple of gentlemen in top-boots, one Squire Stourton of Stourton Castle, and he in a claret coat, cracking a whip, and shouting:

"Clear a road for the happy pair! Clear the way, or I'll cut you across your faces."

"Clear the course, or be—to you all!" shouted George, commonly designated Captain Stracey, who was armed with a silver-headed walking-cane, with which he belaboured such as stood in the way.

"Come along to Stewponey and drink to their healths and happiness!" roared the Squire.

Then forth issued Luke Francis and Bladys.

The latter walked as in a dream, her face colourless, her eyes glazed. She paid no regard to the congratulations showered on her, nor returned the salutations offered, nor did a particle of colour mount to her cheek at the coarse sallies that flew about her. She walked uncertainly, and unless Francis had guided her, she would have stepped off the path and into a bush.

"No bells!" exclaimed the tipsy Lewis Falcon; "Odds boddikins! I don't hold it a proper wedding without b—b—bells."

"Bells!" echoed Stourton. "Gad! We'll have the dinner-bell; well thought on, Lewis. You take my whip and sweep a way among 'em, and I'll fetch it in the twinkling of a marline-spike."

Then, surrendering the hunting-whip to the tipsy youth, he ran into the Castle.

A minute had scarcely elapsed before he returned blowing a Saxhorn, that he held in one hand, and clanging a bell with the other.

The people cheered. Falcon cracked his whip. A boy started out of the crowd and twanged a Jews' harp; but not a sound of this feeble instrument could be heard in the universal din.

Thus the procession moved, drifted, tumbled along, on the way to the inn; some of those in it treading on the heels of the others, now falling and being trodden on by those behind—laughter, screams, oaths, jests, blasphemies, together with the clangour of the bell, the braying of the horn, and the cracking of the whip, forming an indescribable hubbub.

At the tavern door appeared the landlord, waving his cap in one hand, flourishing a tankard of ale in the other, and spilling the contents over those near. He had not attended his daughter to Stourton. He had asked the Squire to act as his deputy and give her away. He knew that eating and drinking would follow on the return of the rabble, and he had to provide accordingly.

"Well, Bla!" shouted he to his daughter, with boisterous mirth, "I wish you joy. It's right the parent should show the way to the child that it should walk in; but, by George, you have distanced me, and given me the go-by. I shan't be long after you."

Bladys looked up at him, but said nothing, neither was there intelligence in her eyes. Even he was struck at her appearance, and asked, in a low tone.

"Does aught ail thee, wench?"

She made no reply, and passed within.

"Come here, son Luke, as I must now entitle thee. And so you have resolved to leave at once?"

"I must be off. My duty exacts my presence at Shrewsbury."

"A deed to be engrossed?"

"No—executed."

"And you start to-night?"

"The day is closing in. Half-an-hour is the most I can allow. I must sleep at Bridgenorth, that I may be in Shrewsbury in good time tomorrow."

The Stewponey was like to a hive into which a wasp has penetrated. The open space in front was dense with people; the interior was packed with them. The bowling-green, the yard, the stables, every portion of ground belonging to it was swarming. People, unable to endure the crush and heat within the house, worked their way out, and simultaneously another stream was intent on forcing its way within, where ale and spirits were thought to be obtainable without charge. Outside the rabble was as in a dance. Men, women, dived in and out amongst the rest in quest of friends and acquaintants. Knots were formed, then dispersed when a drawer appeared bearing refreshment. Then at once a rush ensued that upset him—or his supplies—amidst curses and laughter and outcries.

Tobacco smoke curled in the air; tongues chattered. A boy who had climbed an elm fell with the branch on which he had planted himself and was saved from hurt by knocking down three women and a man, on whose heads and shoulders he tumbled.

A Savoyard with a hurdy-gurdy and a monkey arrived and formed a nucleus around which the young congregated, and not the young only. The sallies of the red-coated ape, its grimaces, produced general mirth and some disturbance.

"Now then! Make room! Now then! Do you want to be run over?"

Clack! clack! went the whip of a post-boy, and a yellow-bodied carriage was brought out of the yard, drawn by two horses, and mounted by a boy in a yellow jacket, white hat, and breeches and top-boots.

When this appeared, for a while attention was diverted from the ape, and the cluster that had formed round the hurdy-gurdy was broken up.

An avenue was opened with difficulty, to allow the horses to draw the vehicle to the inn door.

Then a scream rang out ear-piercingly.

The ape had made a grip at a youth's head of hair as the lad revolved to see the post-boy and carriage, and, what is more, with malicious blinkings and with tenacity the creature retained its hold. The young fellow clutched and struggled to free himself mad with terror. Some of those standing by applauded the monkey and bade him pull harder. Others attempted to release the boy by plucking at the chain attached to the beast's collar.

Instantly the monkey set up his crest of hair, mouthed, growled, and leaped at those who tweaked his chain. This scattered them like chaff and some in their attempt to escape the monkey got under the legs of the horses. The post-boy used his whip on the backs of such as came within reach of his lash, and cast at them the most abusive expletives. The chain had been wrenched from its hold. The monkey was free, and the Savoyard, striving to forge his way after it, joined in the hubbub, dominating the uproar by his shrill cries that Jacko was loose, interlarded with oaths in Italian and entreaties in broken English.

The ape, conscious that it was free, with cunning dropped out of sight to the ground, tucked up the chain, and dived in and out among the feet and petticoats of the crowd, who sprang apart, as though the earth had gaped, whenever they became aware of its proximity. Every now and then it ran up the back of some shrieking individual to take a look round, then jumped down again.

After the ape, as well as he was able to judge his direction, came the Italian, crying out for his Jacko, now appealing to the beast's sense of gratitude, then invoking the assistance of the crowd, then calling down imprecations on all alike.

He was torn, distracted, by alarm lest he should lose his monkey and by solicitude for his instrument, that was subjected to jolts and crushing by the crowd.

None attended to the Italian; all were on the look-out to escape from the hoofs of the post-horses, the wheels of the carriage, or the hands of the ape. Then—none knew exactly when, not at all how—Jacko ceased to provoke uneasiness. He was gone, whither none asked, where none cared, glad to be relieved of menace from him.

The alarm of the rabble abated. They formed hedges, leaving an open way for the travelling carriage, and the post-boy drew up before the inn door. At the same moment the bride and bridegroom appeared in the entrance—he triumphant, with a flame in his bold, dark eyes and a flush on his cheeks, she white as death, impassive, inanimate, some women said indifferent.

Cornelius followed, his bloated face gleaming as a poppy. In his hand was a leather bag.

"By gad, it's heavy," said he, "and ought to be. A good take to-day. Help you on with the housekeeping. All to-day's profits in silver and about fifty in gold in a canvas bag to itself. It shan't be said my daughter has left the Stewponey like a beggar. But, i' fecks, I don't half like your leaving at this time of the evening, and with all this money. The roads are not safe."

"Safe enough for me," said Luke.

"There have been highwaymen about. Not afraid?"

"I! I afraid of highwaymen!" scoffed Francis. "I should consider rather that they would fear me."

"Ah! the law, the law! All well enough in a town, but no protection in the country."

"I have a pair of loaded pistols in the chaise. If any man come to the window without leave, I shall add a dab of lead to his already stupid brain."

"You know best. Where is Captain Stracey?"

"Captain George!" shouted those near, but there was no answer.

"Haven't seen him since we left Stourton," said the Squire.

"We must start," said Luke, and the ostler opened the door of the travelling carriage.

"By George," laughed Rea, and drew himself up, "my daughter's marriage is like that of a lady—with a carriage and pair, and driving away for a honeymoon."

"You haven't put the money bag on the pistols?" asked Francis.

"Not such an ass. The pistols are at top."

"Jacko! Who has seen, stole my Jacko?" cried the Savoyard, running forward.

"Be hanged with your Jacko; stand back," said the landlord. "Now then," to the post-boy. "Tom, off!"

The postillion cracked his whip, the horses pranced and dashed ahead.

Then from the spectators rose a cheer. It was repeated, again repeated. The maids looked from the windows and waved kerchiefs and aprons. The vicar, already in the tavern, smoking, stumbled to the door, and waving his three-cornered hat in one hand and his clay pipe in the other, shouted—

"It's a mad wedding, my masters."

"It is one of your making," said the evening lecturer, who was outside.

"Ah! Brother Priest! and a merry one—because mine. If yours, 'twould have been dull—deadly dull. My masters—it is a mad wedding."

CHAPTER VII. — STAND! DELIVER!

The post carriage from the Stewponey was one the like of which is never seen at the present day, although on the Continent, in places, some venerable survivals linger on to excite our astonishment and amusement.

It was a calash constructed to hold two persons only, with a hood something like that of a hansom, and glazed in front. It was perched on enormous wheels behind, those in front being disproportionately small. The body of the vehicle was swung on immense C springs. It was painted the colour of a marigold, the back being black.

This carriage was far from being incommodious. Although there was no third seat within, there was a bracket on which any such article as a reticule could be placed, but only retained if tied there. No box seat for a driver obstructed the view. Those within commanded a prospect of the scenery, interrupted only by the bobbing form of the post-boy. The powerful springs and the massive construction of the vehicle were of necessity at a period when the roads were unscientifically made and badly kept up.

Throughout the Middle Ages, and down to the beginning of the present century, stones of all kinds and sizes, picked up anywhere, off the fields, dug out of quarries, gathered from water-courses, were thrown over the highways, and thrust into ruts without an attempt being made to reduce their size. It is now considered a primary law that a roadway should be convex in structure, so that the water falling on it may run off at once and be carried away at the water table. No such law was then known. The traffic of horses in the middle wore away the centre, and the section of the road was concave, so that all the mud and water settled in the middle, and resolved the way into one great slough.

A journey over such roads was almost as bad as one along a torrent-bed. It consisted in an alternation between bouncing over boulders and dragging through mire. Nothing was more usual than the fracture of a spring, or the embedding of the wheels in a profound rut, from which the horses were powerless to lift the carriage.

In the neighbourhood of Kinver, where sandstone prevails, and the only alternative is conglomerate, there is no proper material for "metalling" roads. Nor does the river Stour brawl down from mountains, and roll hard pebbles along its bed.

Consequently, notwithstanding that the roads which met and crossed at the Stewponey were of first importance, one being the great artery of communication with Ireland, yet all were equally bad.

When the ruts in the highway became dangerous, then carriages and coaches were driven on the turf at the side, so long as that held together; but when that had been resolved into a quagmire, then the welted roadway had again to be resorted to as preferable.

On our macadamised and steam-rolled roads we spin along as if on ice. A hundred years ago travelling on the king's highway was slow, laborious, and painful. A short journey sufficed to resolve the lily-white human body into a purple and yellow mass of bruises.

For the first half-mile, to keep up appearances, the post-boy maintained a rapid pace by constant application of the whip, and by much objurgation; but as soon as the Stewponey and Stourton Castle were out of sight, he relaxed his energies, and the horses perfectly understood that no more violent exercise was required of them. Their master's carriage, its springs, its wheels, its axle were to be considered, and they subsided into their normal pace, one which a lusty man might have surpassed, by exerting himself, in walking.

"The moon is rising," said Luke Francis. "See, our honey-moon!"

If so—it presaged a cold and cheerless state.

Through the trees glimmered a sallow light. The sun was setting, and setting in torn and tattered cloud, but it diffused light sufficient to render the lesser orb wan and ghost-like. She appeared as lifeless as the bride.

Opposite to the rising moon was the sinking sun, like Hercules in his riven robe of Nessus, all shreds of blood and fire. His face was like that of the bridegroom, flushed with triumph and passion.

"I have been for five years seeking about to find a wife, and unable to get one," said he. "Dost know the reason?"

She evinced no interest in the matter. She neither spoke nor looked towards him.

"You will discover in good time. When we come to Shrewsbury, you will come to know my mother. She has a will. Have you one? I doubt it—so much the better. Your submission will cost no clash, give no pain. Come, wench, your hand—ay, and I will have more—a kiss."

Bladys recoiled from him, withdrew her hand as he extended his, and thrust hers behind her.

"Shy, are you?" he laughed. "Bah! we must have none such whimsy-whamsies now. I should have supposed that in a tavern every trace of shamefacedness had been laughed out of you. But women are made up of pretences. You are affecting that which by the nature of things you cannot have."

She offered no remark.

"Come, now, Bla, by heaven, I will have the hand that is mine."

He made an effort to secure it.

"Let go," said she hoarsely. It was the first word she had spoken.

He tried to kiss her.

The carriage lurched, and he was flung back.

"Do not touch me," she said, in the same unnatural voice.

"Ho, ho! Giving yourself high airs! That will never answer with me. I shall have a kiss."

He laid hold of her shoulders to twist her about.

"I will take them," said he. "One—two—twenty—a hundred. The more I shall take if you resist."

"God help me!" through her teeth.

"You fool!" mocked he. "Do you know with whom you try your petty opposition? No; but you shall learn that soon. Mark you, wench, it is best that you submit at once. Call not on God."

"Heaven has not helped me—I call on Hell." Then it was that a strange thing took place; something that made Luke Francis quail.

This was none other than the sudden apparition of a small, black, half-human figure, that emerged from the boot, as if in answer to the invocation of Bladys. It mounted the little shelf opposite, facing the travellers, blinked, drew up its gums, displaying white fangs, then uttered a low strange guttural growl. It looked at Bladys, and put forth a long arm, and spread forth a black hand.

Neither Francis nor Bladys had seen or heard anything of the Savoyard and his monkey. The sudden vision in the carriage before them turned their hearts to stone. They conceived that an evil spirit was before them.

Instantly recovering himself somewhat, Luke threw open the window on his side, and yelled to the post-boy, "For God's sake, stop! Stop!"

This was just after the carriage had reached a smooth piece of road, and the man had urged the horses to a fast trot. He now reined them in; but without waiting for the carriage to be brought to a standstill, Francis had flung himself out, and holding the open door, ran alongside, crying.

"Stop, boy! What is it? In the name of everything that is holy, what can it be?"

The postillion succeeded in arresting the horses. He descended from the saddle, and came round to where Luke stood.

Within, cowering in the extreme corner, was Bladys, her white face faintly discernible, like the moon, and her hands uplifted to shut out from her the sight of the imp that she had conjured up.

That imp was mouthing and jabbering. It stood up, reseated itself, drew up a chain, shook it, and dropped it tinkling again.

"It is a devil," said Francis.

"It is the monkey," laughed the post-boy. "Whoever would have supposed it had concealed itself here?"

"A monkey!"

"The Italian's Jacko, about which he raised such an outcry."

"A monkey! Is that all? Then I'll drive out the pestilent beast forthwith."

At once Luke put his hands to the creature, but the ape flew at him, bit, clawed, screamed, and Francis found some difficulty in disengaging himself. He cursed, and shook his hand, that bled—he had been bitten in the thumb, and the lappet of his holiday coat was torn.

"Deliver!"

A deep voice in his ear.

Francis started back as one electrified.

He saw surrounding him five men, masked, with swords at their sides and pistols in their hands. At once, aware that he had to do with highwaymen, he made a dash to enter the carriage and get possession of his firearms. But the man who had spoken thrust himself in the way, intercepting him.

"No," said he. "You have saved us trouble by leaving the coach without obliging us to stop it and invite you to descend. Deliver without ado and go on your way with the girl."

"I have nothing," said Francis, recovering self-possession, but speaking in surly mood.

"Nay, that will not avail with us. We know you."

"You know me? Who am I?"

The men laughed.

"Have you not been married to-day? Have you not got your wife's dower with you? Fifty pounds in gold and the rest in silver? You see we know all."

"That is what you know," said Luke, with something of relief in his tone, but also with a spice of mockery.

"What more would you have us know?"

"Oh, certainly, nothing more."

"You have the money with you in a leather wallet. Pardon me, Stewponey Bla, if I disturb you, and excuse the intrusion on you at such a time. I must obtain possession of that bag. Hold him, two of you, whilst I search the interior of the calash. And you, Number Nick, point the pistol to his ear, and if he make a movement, do not scruple to blow out his brains. Unless I am vastly mistaken, the bride will not cry her eyes out to lose him."

Luke bit his lips. But for the apparition of the ape, he would not have left the carriage. Had he been in his place, before the horses could have been arrested, he would have had time to get the pistols, and when the men came to the door, he would have shot two of them dead. That wretched monkey had been the means of delivering him over, unarmed, unable to offer the least resistance, into their hands.

"May I request you to step out?" said one of the highwaymen to Bladys.

He offered his hand.

At once she descended from the carriage, and stood in the road.

Francis looked around him. The carriage had been drawn up where the highway crossed a tract of sandy common strewn with whin bushes and dotted with birch-trees, the former black as blots, the latter silver-trunked and feather-headed. In the rear was a sombre belt of wood, probably Stourton Forest. The man who had handed out Bladys now entered the calash, and removed the pistols and the bag that contained the money.

"These," said he, handing the firearms to one his companions, "these barking irons are more like to render service to us than to the gentleman who has so kindly brought them here. Now, sir, unless the Captain has any more commands for you, when it pleases you to go forward we will not interfere with your will."

The sun had disappeared. A yellow halo hung over the place where he had set, and the moon had mounted above the mists, and displayed her orb lustrous as burnished silver. Every birch trunk stood out as a thread of moonlight.

"My Jacko! My Jacko!" called a voice, and up came the Savoyard, out of breath, "Where my Jacko? Me thought him with carriage. He clebber—me run!"

The man paid no attention to the masked foot-pads. Nothing concerned him save his ape. At his voice the creature that was cowering on the ground uttered a scream of recognition; it had arrived at the conclusion that it was safer with its master than elsewhere. It ran to him and leaped on his shoulder.

"Comrades," shouted the man who acted as leader of the band, "a wedding party this—and no dance. That should never be. I am sorry, my good sir, further to delay you, but such an occasion as this is not of nightly occurrence, and it is a maxim in life to seize opportunities as they pass—take a purse when you can, stop a coach when there is money in the mails, and foot it when there is a partner to be had. Here we have a smooth turf, as any parquet, a musician with his instrument, and the bonny bride herself with whom I shall do myself the honour of opening the ball. Run some one of you, and constrain Nan Norris to come. By Saturn, Mercury, and all the gods of Olympus! I would another carriage might arrive, that we were able to provide ourselves with a lady apiece."

Two men held Luke Francis by the arms, and one pointed a pistol at his head. He was incapable of resistance. He was constrained to look on, quivering with rage, gnawing his lips with vexation. Bladys mechanically obeyed the Captain, as he ordered her to come forward upon the turf. The Italian turned the wheel of his hurdy-gurdy, and fingered the short, bone keys.

Then the monkey, hearing the familiar strain, and supposing that it was expected to go through its wonted performance, somewhat reluctantly descended from its perch, and began to dance.

Presently up came the only disengaged highwayman, bringing with him a young woman. "Nan," called the Captain, "fall in as well." She stood opposite the man who had brought her, and so they danced in the moonlight on the sward—the two highwaymen, the maidens, and, as a fifth, the ape.

Thus they danced, to the grinding of the hurdy-gurdy, till suddenly sank on the grass unconscious.

The highwaymen vanished as speedily as they had appeared. In the chequered light and shade on the common, studded with clumps of whin, birch, ridges and mounds of bramble, this was of easy execution. It would have been so had they been alarmed. But there was now nothing to alarm them— they disappeared because there was nothing more to be got by staying. No sooner was Luke released than he ran to the prostrate girl. Nan Norris also hastened to her assistance.

The Savoyard ceased turning the handle of his hurdy-gurdy. The monkey desisted from its capers, and returned to its place on his shoulder.

The post-boy stood looking on, as stolid as his horses. In the grey light from the sky—partly moonlight, partly the suffused illumination of departed day—the face of Bladys was that of death.

"It is in the family," said the man by the horses. "Her aunt dropped just like this, and died right away."

Nan, who knelt by her head, and was chafing her hands, said, "She may be dead now."

"It is a faint," said Luke. "Help get her into the carriage. We must drive forward, and that without delay."

"Drive forward with her in this condition!" exclaimed the girl. "It's murder."

"Egad, were it not most prudent for me to conduct you both back to the Stewponey?" observed the post-boy.

"To the Stewponey!" echoed Francis. "Never! What, and let all there see, and laugh to see, that I have been robbed! I—I been robbed. On my life, never!"

He stamped with rage.

"Hold your fool's tongue," he continued; "he wins who last laughs, and i' faith they have not done with me yet. 'Twas the worst night's work they ever accomplished when they stayed me. I shall not be balked of my revenge." Then, turning on the girl, he asked, "Do you know—doubtless you do that—who these footpads are? For one fetched you."

"One fetched me—yes; a man masked. But I have no keener eyes than yourself to see through a patch of velvet. I warrant ye I was too scared to disobey when he said, 'Come along with me, baggage.'"

"But you danced."

"So did she—Bla of the Stewponey. She is your wife now, I hear. So did the ape. Ask her when she fetches to—and if she does not, then inquire of the ape."

"I must hurry forwards. I cannot tarry here."

"Then go on, and leave her here."

"What—on this moor?"

"No, not so. Our cottage is hard by."

"Old Lydia Norris has a tavern nigh this," explained the post-boy, "and Nan is her daughter."

Luke hesitated what to do. He was in the utmost perplexity. He could not allow Bladys to remain longer unconscious on the grass in an open common. He was impatient to be away from a spot where he had been robbed and exposed to humiliation. He could not be certain whether his wife were alive or only in a dead syncope. He had pressing duties that necessitated his presence in Shrewsbury.

"Well, it shall be so, then," said he. "I will take her to your house. You have cordials—brandy. We will give her some and see if that revives her, and when she returns to her senses she shall continue the journey."

Then he broke into curses against his misfortune at having been waylaid, and at having been caught at the one moment when he was incapacitated for defending himself and protecting his money.

"You will not recover her by oaths," said the girl. Then to the post-boy, "Prithee, Tom, turn about the heads of the horses, and we will remove her to the Rock."

There was obviously no better course to be taken. Francis acquiesced, sullen and muttering threats. In a very few minutes the postillion drew up where the road was dark, overshadowed by broad-leaved sycamores, so that in spite of all the light of the sky it was there pitch-black night.

On the left hand was a bank, above this bank a garden occupying as it were a terrace above the highway. At the back of the garden a long, low brick cottage. No light shone through the windows.

"Here we are," said Nan. "There is none within, save my old mother. Folk don't come this way after nightfall; our customers are day travellers, and of them only such as are footers. There are three steps at first, then five, and you reach the garden."

"What are your orders for the chaise?" asked the driver. "Shall I unharness?"

"Unharness, you fool!" answered Francis. "Do you not see that there are no stables here? Nowhere that a horse could put his head in? Turn the carriage about. In five minutes my wife will be better and able to resume the journey. What art laughing at?" he inquired sharply, turning on the young woman.

"By Goles, that was purely!" exclaimed Nan. "I was laughing to think that we should have stables, mother and I. Odds boddikins! Whatever should we do with horses?"

Bladys, still unconscious, was conveyed into the cottage. The building was but one room deep, but had a face that showed it comprised three chambers; these were in communication within. The house was constructed against a bank, on the top of which grew sycamores. Wooden shutters were before the windows.

When the door was opened, then it was seen that the tavern was constructed against a face of rock, which served as inner wall, and this face was dug into to form recesses for shelves, and pierced by a door that probably gave access to the cellar.

A fire was seen burning on the hearth, and an old woman sat crouching over it with hands extended, so that the flames threw gigantic shadows on the walls and ceiling.

"What have you here?" croaked the crone. "Nan, I'll have no corpses brought in. Anything but that. I have ever set my face against that. I have no fancy to wear Onion's collar."

Luke Francis started, and looked inquiringly at the speaker.

"Mother," answered the daughter, "this is the Stewponey wench that was married to-day, as you have heard tell. She is ill, in a faint—God knows, perchance dead."

"I'll have no corpses here. They'll inquitch her in the house, and I won't have it. I don't like the look and smell of crowners. They turns my stomick."

Nan explained to Francis, "Mother is a bit hard of hearing, and she's full of old woman's whimsy-whamsies. Don't you heed a word she says."

"Lay my wife by the fire, where she can have warmth. Is there a surgeon near? She may need be let blood."

"I'll have no blood here," screamed Mistress Norris. "Gold—gold, if you will, and welcome, but blood has no profit in it."

Nan helped to place Bladys on the tiled floor by the hearth. The red glow of the turf and wood fire fell over her death-like face.

The mouth was partially open, and the teeth glinted in the firelight. The eyelids were also ajar, and there was a glitter of the white of the balls below the lids.

"Have they shot her or run her through?" called the hag. "I have always said it was folly to shed blood." She leaned forward, and peered at the insensible girl on the floor.

"She is in a faint, mother," said Nan, and took the beldame by the shoulders, twisted her round, and said, "Look to the pot with the taties and bacon boiling for supper, and don't speak another word."

"I don't want to have nothing to say to Onion," persisted the old woman.

"Nor will you, mother. Hold your tongue. We must attend to the guests."

"I won't have no corpses brought here. I hate 'em," said the hag, stamping her foot on the hearth, and then beating with her clenched fist on her knee. "There's the getting rid of them—that's the difficulty. I always said, 'Keep off—'"

"Mother, mind the pot; it's boiling over."

At that moment the doorway was entered by the Savoyard, who pulled off his hat, and, bowing, asked:

"Me here sleep? Take leetle place."

"Do you not see," said Nan Norris, irritably, "that we have the sick woman to attend upon? We cannot receive you. Go your ways farther."

But the monkey had seen the fire. With a leap it reached the floor, ran to the hearth, and jumped upon a stool opposite the old hostess, seated itself and stretched out hands and feet, much as did she, blinking and grinning with pleasure as it enjoyed the heat.

Mistress Norris saw the creature, and fell into an ecstasy of laughter. Her thoughts were diverted from Bladys and riveted on the monkey.

Nan immediately saw the advantage, and signed to the Italian to take a seat by the door.

"Ho, ho! my little Beelzebub!" croaked the hag, "not come for me yet, have you? Rubbing your hands? Have you the soul of that pretty lady in your pouch? Done your job to-day, Beelzebub? Well, well, well, we're all friends together here."

Nan, kneeling beside Bladys, unlaced her stays, applied vinegar to her temples, poured it over her throat. She endeavoured ineffectually to force some drops of brandy into her mouth.

The Savoyard shut the door.

"Leave it open," ordered Nan sharply. "We require the fresh air."

Francis stood by in great unrest and impatience, looking into the face of his inanimate wife. Suddenly Bladys drew a long inspiration, and opened her eyes.

"There!" exclaimed Nan triumphantly, "I knew that she was not gone. She will return to herself shortly. Sit up, my love! Sit up and let me stay thee." Nan put her arms about the hardly conscious girl, and lifted her to a sitting posture.

"Now," said she coaxingly, "take a drop of cordial. It will bring the colour back into your dead lips."

Bladys looked around her with a puzzled expression. Now she fixed her eyes on the young woman who was supporting her, then turned them searchingly on Francis, but instantly averted them, caught sight of the ape in so doing, as it made passes over the fire and grinned and nodded its head at the old mother, who bobbed and laughed in response from the farther side of the fire.

Bladys shivered, turned her head sharply away, and hid her face in Nan's bosom. She trembled in every limb.

"Ho, ho! Beelzebub!" jested the old hostess, who had eyes, thoughts, for nothing save the monkey; "we have always been prime friends, always, and ever shall be, eh?" and she broke into a harsh cackle.

"Can you stand?" asked Nan of Bladys. "Don't mind that creature. It is but a monkey in a red coat. I'll drive it forth out of the house if it affright thee."

"Beelzebub!" laughed the old woman, thrusting a long brown arm through the smoke, signing to the ape with one finger to demand attention.

"We may be returning the civility of this call shortly. There is no telling. They have brought a corpse into the house—a corpse of a young wench—and that may bring us everyone into the hands of Onion. Onion! Whew!" She screamed with laughter. "That 's your master waggoner as brings you consignments of souls, all bound with a hempen halter. Eh, eh?"

Nan, with her arms about the waist of Bladys, had been endeavouring to raise her, assisted by Francis; but something said or done disturbed him to such an extent that his attention was drawn away from his wife, and he allowed the entire burden to fall on the girl. She was strong armed and lusty, and did not let go her hold. Nan now pressed more brandy on Bladys, and persuaded her to swallow a few drops. A point of crimson, like the bursting out of a sudden flame, came in her cheek, but died again as quickly.

"Come now," urged Francis, "time presses. I shall not reach Bridgenorth afore midnight, and there I must sleep, that I may be in Shrewsbury to-morrow, and to-morrow in Shrewsbury I must be."

"The judges are going to Shrewsbury," said the old woman. "Beelzebub, wilt accompany the gentleman? There'll be rare doings at Shrewsbury. Tom Matthews—he is certain sure to be convicted; a good lad, but 'tis a pity. It's a poor trade stealing sheep. Better be hung for cutting a purse than taking a pelt. Ding dong bell! Ring the gallows-bell, and Tom Matthews be the clapper! Eh, Beelzebub?"

Then the aged woman burst again into a hideous cackle, and laid her shrivelled finger on the arm of the monkey.

Bladys shuddered, without understanding what was said, or to what the allusion pointed.

"And further, Beelzebub. There is, they inform me, a sweet creature to be tried for not loving her husband, and for setting her fancy upon another; and she gave her husband a drop of nightshade that sent him below. Ho, ho; if she had but consulted me, I could have better advised her. They assure me that for this they will burn her."

The old woman rubbed her palms over the fire.

"I have never seen a woman at the stake. Ecod, I should prodigiously like to see that. But this kind gentleman will not deny me such a trifle if I ask him to take me with him. And she to be burnt alive! That's pure. I should enjoy myself extravagantly."

"Stand up now," said Francis to his bride. "Try if you can walk to the chaise. Positively we must press on. I have been delayed too considerably."

Entreaty, command, availed nothing. The limbs of the hardly conscious and enfeebled girl would not support her. She dragged in his arms and those of Nan, and would have sunk in a heap on the floor had they not sustained her entire weight.

"Curses fall on it," swore Luke. "What the foul fiend is to be done? I must go on my way. I cannot, I dare not, tarry. Most important matters call me. She must and she shall come."

"She can not," said Nan firmly, "and I swear to your face she shall not. If you attempt to take her along with you she will die in the chaise, and when you reach Bridgenorth it will be along with a corpse."

"I'll have no corpses here," yelled the hag.

"Carry her to the carriage. Then they'll inquitch her in that, and welcome; but not here. I won't have no crowning in my house; it goes against my stomick!"

"I cannot leave her here," said Luke, stamping and taking a turn round the room with his hand to his head. "Was there ever so fatal a situation? Here am I robbed and my wife half dead, and I summoned away. I must go. It is as much as my place is worth to be absent. I have delayed over-long."

He came again before Bladys. "Make an effort to reach the carriage," he said.

She tried to speak, could not, and seemed rapidly relapsing into insensibility.

"Zounds!" said Luke, "what is to be done? I cannot leave her here."

"Why not?" asked Nan, looking him level in the eyes. "Dost think we're not honest folk? I trow we're every whit as honest as you. Go your way; you've nought to fear. You've been robbed, and have nothing further to lose on the main toby (highway). Trust her to me. I will take care of her. You can come when you list, and fetch her away. But if you try to remove her, by Goles! You'll have to use force, and I'll try my nails on your face. I have heard of Bla of the Stewponey, though I never knew her. The Stewponey is a great house, and ours is a main little one. We have not lived vastly far apart. I have never heard aught but good spoken of her. Go on your ways—to Shrewsbury if you must. She shall be cared for, never mistrust it."

"If this must necessarily be so," said Luke; and still he was unable to reconcile his mind to this alternative. "But—" he did not finish the sentence.

"If this must necessarily be so—" said Nan; and gently laid Bladys again on the floor, then went through the doorway, deliberately removed the wooden shutter that closed the window, and let the light from the room flow through it.

"Now," said she, "Tom and the horses are becoming impatient, and I desire to shut the door."

"Beelzebub!" screamed the old woman. "The gentleman is going, and he has not the civility to take me with him. But I'll go, nevertheless, and thou also, little devil! Ay, sly fox, waiting for me?"

CHAPTER IX. — NAN

Luke Francis had departed; and Nan Norris carried Bladys to bed, and did all that lay in her power to soothe her overwrought nerves, rightly judging that what she needed was not rousing, but the opposite treatment.

She sat by the bed till she saw that Bladys was asleep. Then she descended the stairs, went outside the house, and put up the shutter.

The Savoyard lay by the expiring fire, and was snoring; the monkey, coiled up in a ball in his bosom, was also asleep.

Satisfied with what she had done, Nan now opened the door to an adjoining apartment in the length of the house, and shut that after her. Next she unbolted an outer door, and in another minute the sound was heard of the clatter of horse hoofs up the steps to the garden from the road. Immediately following the sound came the horses that had produced it. They passed in at the door, through the room, and disappeared into a cellar behind, excavated out of the rock.

Five entered, and were followed by as many men wearing masks. The leader threw off his and disclosed the face of George Stracey—the man who had entered for the game of bowls that was to be played for Bladys, but who had withdrawn.

"Give us a buss, wench!" said Stracey; "we've not done badly to-night, but there was no occasion for our horses, as it happened."

"Hush!" said she; "make no noise. We have guests. Did you not mark that the shutter was down?"

"Ay, or we should have stabled our beasts earlier. But you have closed now, and that is the signal that our quarters are safe."

"Jacomo is here."

"There is nothing to be apprehended from him. He is our very good servant, and anon does us an excellent turn."

"And Stewponey Bladys is above."

"Alive or dead?"

"Alive and asleep."

"Od's life! she looked like one dying. You baggage, you were jealous, and would not let me contest for such a prize, or I might have won."

"No, George, I would not permit it."

"You jade! Come now, give us a wet of gin; we're cold with tarrying so long in the falling dew, waiting for notice that all was safe."

"Step into the cellar. Nothing can be heard that is said there."

When morning broke, Stewponey Bla opened her eyes. Nan perceived with delight that she was recovering; there was no longer a dazed look in her eyes, a stony indifference in her face; some colour now flushed her cheeks. Nan had shared her bed with Bladys, and when she rose she addressed her companion in cheery fashion, and was answered rationally and readily. Not only so, but Bladys exhibited a desire to know where she was, and how she came to be there.

"My dear," said Nan, setting her arms akimbo, with a hand on each hip, "you and your man, when you was married yesterday, were travelling to Bridgenorth, and the rascally highwaymen stayed the carriage. Ah me! What a sight of wickedness there is in the world! And that man of yours turned out of the chaise, and emptied his pockets, and surrendered all the blunt he had, mild as butter-milk, and shaking for fear in his shoes." The girl broke into a merry laugh. "By dear Goles! I dare be sworn it is sufficient to frighten any man to see about him masked men; and you—you was also out of your senses. Yet they made you dance with them on the heath. And some of those God-forsaken knaves fetched me also to tread a measure. But I heed them not. I have no gold to lose, nor silver either. They do no harm to the poor, they address their courtesies to the rich alone. As for me, I can hold my own in the face of them. And Toni, the post-boy, he took it all as a matter of course. It isn't the first time Tom has been stopped, I'll warrant ye."

Nan was a handsome girl, short, firmly knit, with high colour, dark hair, and lustrous hazel eyes full of twinkle. As she spoke there was a dash and fire in her manner that plainly said the wickedness of the world did not vastly grieve her, that the world would have been but a dull planet without some spice of wickedness in it, and that highwaymen were not to her objects of utter abhorrence.

"It is well for you that you fainted. Captain Velvetface—"

"Who is Velvetface?"

"The Captain. You see all have black faces—but they are muffled in crape, whereas he alone has a mask of velvet. Oh! a rare man is he!" She flushed and her eyes gleamed. "He might have carried you off. I know Velvetface. That is, I have heard tales told of him. They declare that he loves gold dearly, but that he loves pretty girls more dearly still than gold. Set a bag of yellow guineas before him, and beside it a bright-eyed quean, and I know which he will choose. But you were white and dead, like a figure of snow, and not to his taste. So he chose the money bag. Poor fool," laughed Nan. "I dare swear you have not kissed your husband, and now he has run away."

"He is gone?"

"Gone home to Shrewsbury. The talk is that he is in the law, and the assizes are coming on. Bah!" She wiped one hand against the other. "I would have no dealings with a lawyer. Such be spiders as weave the webs that catch and throttle our boys. Ah, well! we're clear of Onion this year. Tom Matthews is none of ours."

"What do you mean by Onion?"

"Onion? I thought every man, woman, and child knew of him."

"Who is he?"

"The hangman."

"Do you know him?"

"I know of him. That is enough. I' fecks—I pray God deliver me from further acquaintance with him. He wears a mask, they say. I do not know. I have never been at a hanging. He is an Onion, they tell, that has brought tears into many eyes."

Then Nan departed.

When she had left the room Bladys rose. She was weak in body, but composed in mind and clear in head. She was desirous of being alone, for only when alone was she in condition to understand the events that had taken place, and through which she had passed.

During the previous day her mind had been half-dead. She had seen, heard, felt, what had transpired, without any corresponding emotion within. A series of pictures had passed before her eyes, but they had been to her without significance.

The distress and perplexity to which she had been subjected had deprived her of sleep, and had so harassed her by day that she had been thrown into a condition of nervous exhaustion, in which everything was indifferent to her. She had been as a sleep-walker upon the day when she was bowled for, won, and wedded. Her actions had been those of an automaton.

It may be that a swoon is Nature's method of recuperation of the vital powers, that it concentrates into a little space of time the beneficial effects of a week of unintermittent slumber.

The long lapse into unconsciousness, followed by even sleep, had restored the mental activity of Bladys. She was glad to be left alone, that she might review what had taken place and orientate herself for the future.

She dressed slowly, and then seated herself on a stool by the latticed window, looking forth into the foliage of the sycamores, through which the light twinkled, as the morning wind agitated the leaves.

Now she was able to summon before her every picture that had presented itself to her eyes on the day before.

It was as the Witch of Endor calling up ghosts and quaking before the apparitions that answered. The proceedings of the previous day unrolled themselves before her in their proper sequence. She could recall every incident, even the most minute and trifling; every word that had been spoken, even the intonation of the voices that had spoken them. But now, and now only, did she understand what these pictures and utterances signified. As the melody in Baron Munchausen's post-horn was frozen, and at the time it was sounded remained mute, but afterwards, by the fire, became unsealed and the notes flowed in their proper order and harmonic propriety, so was it now with the recollection of the events of the day that was past. As Bladys sat at the window looking at the twinkling foliage, she saw them not, but instead contemplated a retrospect.

Her father had been impatient to be rid of her that he might bring Catherine Barry into the house—one of whom she could not think without a shudder as the element that embittered her mother's last days, the cause of the acceleration of her end. Branded into her convictions was the thought that it would not have been possible for her to remain at the Stewponey when that woman entered it to assume therein a position as mistress.

There was sufficiency of good feeling in her father's dull and perverted heart to make him aware of this. But the manner in which he sought to rid himself of his child was in itself an outrage, hardly inferior to that of introducing Catherine Barry into her mother's room. There was no other excuse for his conduct than the lame one of weakness. And indeed more mischief is worked in the world by feebleness than by vice. This impotence of will had led Cornelius Rea into the scandal of setting his daughter as a prize to be gamed for, and of thrusting her into the arms of a man of whom he knew nothing and for whom she did not care.

She saw before her eyes the bowling-green. She was alone on it with Crispin Ravenhill; she saw his soft eyes full of kindly light, heard the tremor of his voice as he spake kindly to her, felt again the throbbing of her heart in response. And she saw, further, the bowling-green invaded by a great concourse of men; she saw the number of competitors reduced to two, the jack cast, the bowls thrown; she heard once more the controversy over the unbiassed ball, she saw the wrestling men—everything up to the moment when she touched the jack with her foot, set it rolling, and it tripped up Crispin Ravenhill.

Then she sprang to her feet with a cry of dismay, of anguish, of self-reproach; she thrust the fingers of both hands through her dark hair and drew them out as far as she could extend her hair, and stood thus, as one struck to stone.

"What ails thee?" asked Nan, running up the stairs at her cry.

"Nan Norris," said Bladys hastily, "I must know what followed. I have got so far. Listen to me." With feverish heat, with gleaming eyes, and a flame burning in each cheek, she told the girl all that had taken place—she spoke of the events as though reading them out of a book, with breathless rapidity.

And then, when she reached the fall of Crispin, she broke off. Then, after a pause, she said—

"I must know what has happened to him. Is he dead? Did I kill him? Nan, Nan, I will myself go to Kinver and inquire."

"That you cannot, or you shall not do," said the warm-hearted girl.

"Nan, I shall die of self-reproach and dreadful expectations. I cannot endure it. I must know. The thought is like a drop of fire that will not out; it burns in—ever more inward. I must know the truth. I rolled the jack. He tripped and fell—fell with his head on it. If I had not touched the jack, he would not have gone down. He would have been the conqueror, and I—I—" she withdrew her hands from her streaming hair, and covered her face.

"Set your mind at ease," said Nan caressingly. "You'll get mazed with thinking and with fancies. I'll myself run to Kinver, and you shall hear all anon. Sit you down and think no more about it. Yet, this I can tell you; I do not believe he can be dead, or some tidings would have reached our place before now. Bad news goes about like squirrels."

Nan was as good as her word. She threw a shawl over her head and went forth.

During her absence Bladys sat at the window, looking into the twinkling leaves, and with thoughts that twinkled—now flashing with hope, now obscure with despair. She did not move from her place; she did not stir a finger of her folded hands, only her lips moved as she spoke with herself inaudibly.

The time passed without her being able to estimate how long it was. Whether she had been sitting there for ten minutes, for ten years, for an eternity, she could not have said. She was in one of those trances— of which perhaps death may be one—in which time ceases to be an element to be accounted with. She was roused by the hand of Nan on her shoulder.

"Stewponey Bla! He is alive and recovering. He was stunned; nothing worse. By Goles, though, there was something worse—he lost you by that fall."

Bladys looked round at Nan, and said:

"I have something for your ear."

"What may that be?"

Nan threw herself on the floor at the feet of Bladys. She was hot and tired with running, her hair dispersed, her eyes twinkling with pleasure and with kindly thought. She folded her hands on the knee of Bladys, and looked up into her white face.

"Nan, can you answer questions?"

"That depends on what the questions be."

"Nan, I will never, never be the wife of the man who has married me. So help me God."

"Whew!" exclaimed Nan, "and where in all this is the question?"

"What now shall I do?"

"That," said Nan, "is what I cannot answer. You must take mother into counsel; she has teeth to crack such nuts."

CHAPTER X. — CASTLE FOREGATE

On the second day a red-headed, red-whiskered man arrived in a buggy, drawn by a sandy horse with a straw-coloured mane and tail.

He had been commissioned by Luke Francis to fetch Bladys. Business that was urgent prevented Francis from himself coming for her, but he sent word that she might rely on his substitute to convey her to Shrewsbury on the morrow, where he awaited her arrival with the impatience of a lover.

A difficulty arose as to the disposal of the horse. As Nan said, they had no accommodation at the Rock Tavern for beasts; but if the man liked to turn out the horse in a paddock for the night, and himself lie at the inn, they were able to accommodate him so far, as there was a spare chamber.

To this he readily consented, as he desired to start at an early hour on the morrow.

"What is your name?" inquired Nan.

"Abraham—Thomas Abraham," replied the man. The old woman over the fire looked up and said:

"There was an Abraham Jarrock, a boy, and he had a red head, and his father had a red head before him, and he came from Bewdley."

The man drew back out of the light, but the glittering eyes of the old woman followed him.

"You're sure you're not Abraham Jarrock? He was a tiresome boy, and had red hair."

"My name is Thomas Abraham."

"And yet you've a red head."

She turned and rubbed her dry palms over the fire. Presently she looked round and asked:

"You come from Bewdley?"

"No, I do not, but from Shrewsbury."

"And yet you've a red head."

She again ruminated over the fire, rubbing her hands together. Then, after awhile, reverted to the same topic.

"What was your father's head like?"

"Grey," answered the man impatiently.

"And yet yours is red. It may have been red before it turned grey. How do you know that it was not red once?"

"I remember it only grey."

"It may have been red, and then you'd be a Jarrock, and come from Bewdley."

"Don't attend to mother, she has queer maggots in her brain," said Nan.

Next morning betimes Abraham had the buggy at the door, with the sandy horse between the shafts, and was stroking its straw-coloured mane.

Bladys parted from Nan Norris with tears on both sides. The girl had been kind to her, and although Abraham was commissioned to pay what charges were for the entertainment of Bladys and his own lodging, yet no money could discharge the debt of tenderness she owed to this warm-hearted girl.

Bladys mounted beside the driver and started for Shrewsbury. She was pale as heretofore, but otherwise was different in appearance from what she had been on the day of her marriage. The look of vacuity, of listlessness, of indifference was passed away. Now her lips were set, as with firm resolve, and there was a covert glow in her eyes that threatened at the least provocation to flash forth in lightnings.

Abraham found her indisposed for conversation; but he himself was prone to talk, and he endeavoured ineffectually to engage her in conversation. But his efforts were not pleasant: he was of a churlish and acrid disposition, and his thoughts turned mainly in the direction of abuse of every person above him in station, and of every institution of his country. He abused the roads, the magistrates, the tavern where he had lain over-night, and the hostess.

After this had gone on for some time he said, "After all, the old woman was right. I am a Jarrock, my father had red hair, and I come from Bewdley."

"Then why did you deny it?" asked Bladys.

"It is inconvenient to tell everything to everyone who asks."

"Why should it be inconvenient unless there be something that has to be concealed?"

"Oh! you think everybody tells you his name and profession, do you? There may be reasons why both have to be kept back—foolish prejudices exist. You will understand that by-and-by."

"What do you mean by by-and-by?"

"When you reach Shrewsbury."

Bladys said nothing further; she was not concerned about so trifling a matter as the real name of the man who drove her, and the colour of his father's hair.

Jarrock growled his dissatisfaction at the uncommunicativeness of his companion. He set her down in his black list as one of those against whom he entertained a grievance.

Said he presently, "Have you travelled along this road afore?"

"Never."

"Except when coming to be robbed. The master has told me of that. He is in a take-on about it, and hardly knows what course to pursue. On the one hand, if he disclose it, he may become an object of mockery, but then he will secure the rogues who robbed him. But on the other, he would rather bear his loss than expose himself. There is one comfort to him. The rascals do not know whom they lightened of his blunt."

To this also Bladys said nothing.

After a while Abraham proceeded unabashed.

"It is time the net was drawn; it makes a man mad to see how they take one and lay him by the heels, and wait, and do no more. Then into his place steps another. There are gentlemen among them. The last taken was one. You'll see him shortly."

"Is he at Shrewsbury?"

"My child, no—on the road to it; strung up, two years ago. We pass the gallows."

Bladys shuddered.

"'Twas brought home in a curious way. The gentleman he robbed had been in Wales and had shot an eagle, so he had a claw set in gold for a pin to his cravat. When he was stayed in his carriage by foot-pads, one of them clicked his pistol at his head, for he struggled hard, but the pistol would not go off. Good for him. So the highwayman made free with the gentleman's pin to pick the nipple of his piece, thinking it choked, and forgot to return it. Two nights after, the squire who had been stopped was at the Assembly Rooms at Wellington at a county ball there, and in the country dance, who should be opposite him in the set, but a gent with an eagle's claw set in gold in his cravat! He seized him there, and no escape was possible. He was taken and tried at the next assizes and—Look up. There is the gibbet, and there he hangs."

Bladys, in horror, raised her hands to screen from her eyes the ghastly object suspended by the wayside; she averted her head, but could not shut her ears to the croak of the crows that swarmed about the gallows and sat on the cross-beam.

"What?" laughed Abraham. "Don't you like to see that? Well, that's queer, and you're strangely made. When Adam Bell was slung by the neck for shooting Squire—dang me if I recall the name—to obligate the family they put the gallows where it could be seen from the withdrawing-room windows. That was by special request of the ladies. You—when you arrive at Shrewsbury—have a real treat awaiting you, such as you have not a chance of seeing often."

He paused, expecting to be asked to explain. As, however, Bladys exhibited no curiosity, he continued in a churlish tone:

"There's no pleasing some folks. If you give them simnel cake, they will say they prefer mince pies; and if you offer them roast loin of mutton, they'll say, 'We eat only furmity.' I'll tell you what to expect. There is a woman going to be burnt at Shrewsbury—none of your common sort, but a real gentlewoman. She was wed to a man she did not love, and she loved another. She endeavoured to rid herself of the husband, so as to go off with the lover, and she poisoned her goodman. But it was discovered. That is what we call petty treason. Never heard of that before? I'll explain it to you. If a woman destroys her husband, or a servant murders his master, that is petty treason; a man is hung and drawn for it, a woman is burned. The gentlewoman—she came from a place called Nesscliffe—was tried the day before yesterday at the assizes, and was found guilty, and condemned to be burned. There will be a multitude of people from all round to see it. Pray heaven it may be a fine day. That is not a sight you will have the luck to see at Kinver," Abraham continued, regardless of the repugnance to hear this talk manifested by Bladys:

"We have had women hanged. There is nothing out of the common way in that. But petty treason does not occur as frequently as it might. As to hanging—now, they do not leave women as they do men to swing till they drop. We had a young woman hung here last assizes at Shrewsbury for borrowing her mistress's gown and hat to go to the fair with her fancy lad, and there happened to be a guinea missed as well. But she was cut down after she was dead, and before she was cold. She had a neck like a swan. There's more satisfaction in hanging one who has a long neck, but there is more art in dealing with your bull necks. That man we have just passed had no more throat than a toad. When he was turned off, there was no getting him properly strangled, so there was nothing for it but to jump on his shoulders."

"I entreat you to be still!" exclaimed Bladys. "If you will persist in thus talking, I will leave the carriage."

The man turned about in his seat and stared at her, and burst into a roar of laughter.

"Well! this is rare, and you his wife!"

Bladys did not speak, her lips turned white, and a shudder passed through her at a thought which traversed her brain. Her eyes were fixed on the flapping mane of the trotting horse. Abraham, sulky at being unable to engage her in conversation, or to interest her in his narratives, fell into silence.

Questions rose in the mind of Bladys as bubbles in fermenting wine, yet not a word passed over her lips. At length the condition of uncertainty in which she was became unendurable, and she said, hesitatingly, in a low voice, without withdrawing her eyes from the straw-coloured mane.

"Your name is not Thomas Abraham?"

"It is Abraham. My father was called Thomas. I might have called myself Thomson, being an Englishman, or Ap Thomas had I been Welsh."

"You have another name?"

"Yes; I am Abraham Jarrock."

"And he—Luke Francis?"

"The Master?"

"Yes; the Master."

"What of him?"

"Has he also another name to Luke Francis?"

"These be his Christian names."

"I thought as much. And what is his surname?" The fellow hesitated. Then he shrugged a shoulder, whipped the horse, and said.

"Onion."

Bladys made no remark.

A long pause followed. Then again she spoke. "You are his servant?"

"On no account. I am his assistant."

"In what trade?"

"That you shall learn presently. He laid it on me as an obligation to keep silence. But be not concerned. When we reach Shrewsbury you shall know all."

She said no more.

After awhile the day began to close. They were approaching their destination. The road was no longer without traffic. They passed the half-ruined Abbey, and here a crowd was assembled in an open space before the west front of the stately church. It was watching the proceedings of some workmen.

Abraham chuckled and, nudging Bladys, said, "Dost know what they are about? Preparing for to-morrow. The woman will be burnt there—she I told you of child, who married one man and loved another."

Then they crossed the "English Bridge" over the Severn, and saw the town, with its walls and old houses, and church towers rising steeply beyond the red river.

Abraham drew his hat down so as to conceal his face.

A drift of men in livery bearing white wands went by.

"There goes the sheriff attended by his javelin men: we must move aside," said Jarrock; "he goes to inspect the place of execution."

The street was alive with people following the sheriff and his retinue, or hanging round a ballad singer, or clustering together to discuss some point of interest or controversy.

A woman was bawling out the information that she had for sale the last confession of the murderess, price one penny, the whole set forth in rhyme.

Then she chanted in a cracked voice:

"Come all you feeling-hearted Christians, wherever you may be.
Attention give to these few lines, and listen unto me.
It's of a cruel murder to you I will unfold;
The bare recital of the same will make your blood run cold.

Confined within a lonely cell with sorrow thus oppressed.
The very thought of what I've done deprives me of my rest.
Within this dark and gloomy cell in the county gaol I lie.
For murdering of my husband dear I am condemned to die!"

The clog in the street occasioned by the passage of the sheriff was removed; Jarrock drove on. The street had ascended; now it descended rapidly. The walls and machicolations of the Castle rose against the evening sky, and the glow of departing daylight made the red walls doubly red.

Abraham pointed to the town gate, below the Castle, a gate with a chamber above it and over that, in a sort of tower, a large bell. At the side of the gate was a door.

"Step down," said Jarrock; "your home is here—here in the Hangman's house!"

CHAPTER XI. — A WHITE DEVIL

A small nail-studded oak door opened into a dwelling-house by the side of the gate, a dwelling which apparently extended over it. A flight of five steps led to this door. In the doorway stood an old woman, tall, with a black shawl drawn over her iron-grey hair. She had thin, strongly-marked features, eyes set unduly near her nose, and these hard, the irises like polished agates. Her lower jaw was strong, prominent, and the mouth large and unfurnished with lips. As she held a candle over her head in order to see Bladys, her own sharp ungainly features were illumined.

She admitted the girl at once, and fastened the door behind her, then proceeded to ascend the stairs before her to a chamber on an upper floor, level with that above the gate with which it communicated. Then she put the candle on the table and looked steadily at Bladys by its light and that of a wood fire.

"You are white," said the woman.

"I am always white," said the girl.

"And cold?"

"Always cold unless angered—then, fire."

"I am the mother of Luke," said the old woman. "He is out at present, but will be home shortly. You are hungry. I have spread the table. Will you sup?"

Bladys seated herself.

"Yes," she said, composedly, "I can eat."

"Eat at once. I cannot say at what hour my son returns. This is his busy time."

The old woman watched Bladys attentively as she ate, not without marvel at her self-possession. She leaned one sharp elbow on the table, and with her bony hand shaded her eyes whilst she studied the new inmate of the Gate House.

"How old are you?" she inquired.

"I am one and twenty."

"Ah! you are not troubled with diffidence. You come from a tavern?"

"Where I have learned to hold at a distance such as are disposed to be forward."

"You know to what house you have come?"

"I know."

"You know what is the name of my son?"

"I know."

"You know what is his trade?"

"I know."

"And that does not trouble you?"

"Oh! no."

"Have you any notion what my son is engaged upon now, that he is not here to receive you?"

Then Bladys laid her knife on the table, and looked across the table into the stony eyes of the woman, and said:

"He is planting the stake, and is heaping up the faggots, for the burning of a woman to-morrow, who was married to a man against her consent, and who put him away. And there is an iron hoop that is affixed to that stake which is to surround her waist, and hold her upright in the flames, and retain her lest she attempt to break away. And your son is hammering in the staples that make the hoop fast."

Then she resumed her knife and continued to eat.

The old woman raised her eyebrows. A look of perplexity, like a film, passed over her beady irises.

When Bladys had eaten, she stood up.

"You bid no blessing on your food," said Mrs Onion.

"No blessing can come on it in this house."

"And you have given no thanks after it."

"To whom?"

"To God."

"It is no gift of God, it is the meat of the hangman."

The old woman rose.

"I will show you to your chamber," she said. "But tell me. What think you of my son Luke? He is a fine man, a handsome fellow."

Bladys made no reply. The woman repeated the question.

"What think you of Luke?"

"I think of him only as the hangman." Again the mother turned to stare at her. "Come now, child, I am his mother, and yet you have not kissed me."

"No, I will not."

"And wherefore not?"

"Because you are the hangman's mother."

"But I am your mother now."

"My mother is dead."

The old woman laughed.

"You will kiss my son, my handsome son, readily enough."

"No, I will not."

"He will kiss you."

"That he shall not."

"You are my son's wife."

"I am his servant."

"You are right in that," sneered Mrs Onion. "She who is his wife is his servant also."

"I did not say—his servant also. I am his servant, and that only."

"Come, now, this is arrant folly. I will show you to your room."

"That cannot be my room. It is the hangman's room. Give me a chamber to myself as befits a servant."

"We shall soon see to this," exclaimed the mother, in concentrated white rage. "What sort of woman are you that Luke has brought home?"

"He did not bring me hither. That did his assistant, Abraham Jarrock; and he brings to this house one other than she whom your son married. He was wed to a frightened girl, thrust forth from her father's house, made an object of jest, the prize of a game at bowls. But that is not the woman who comes here tonight"

"How so?"

"He did not win me, that did another."

"Oh—was it so?"

"And that other who won me, I love."

"Is it so?" jeered the mother.

"And to that other alone will I give myself."

"Hah! Take the candle; hold it on high, that I may look well into your face."

Bladys did as was desired. Elevating the light, she held it steadily, so as to let her white cold face be flooded by it. The features were set, the mouth firm, the eyes resolved.

"You are my son Luke's wife," said Mrs Onion; "that you cannot change. That which is done, cannot be undone."

"He married me without giving his true name."

"Luke Francis is his name."

"He married me without telling his profession."

"That matters nought."

"I will never be his wife."

"Then why did you come to this house?"

"I had nowhere else whither I could go. I will be the hangman's servant, but I will not be his wife."

"Pshaw!" said the old woman. "They have scared you like a child. They have represented my son as a bugbear. He is a good man and reads his Bible, and I am a religious woman. Why should he be worse than the judge that condemns? than the jury who convict? than the men who make the laws? He doth but execute what they order. His is the hand that performeth what the head directeth. We are given free lodgings, and are paid; and, moreover, we have a right to the clothing of such as are sent to their death by the hands of Luke. If there be crime, must it not be punished? And is he not worthy of esteem who executes the decree upon the criminal? What would the world come unto save violence and savagery if it were not that Justice stands forth to protect the weak? My son is but the minister of Justice. What saith the Scripture? 'Wilt thou not be afraid of the power, do that which is good. For he is the minister of God to thee for good. But if thou do evil, be afraid, for he beareth not the sword in vain; he is the minister of God, a revenger to execute wrath upon him that doeth evil.' What are you, to scorn what the Word of Scripture deemeth honourable?"

"I am content to be his servant," said Bladys. Mrs Onion had opened the door to lead from the room; she shut it again with impatience, and returned to the table and placed the candle upon it.

"This is perversity," she said. "His wife you are, to love, honour, and obey; and his wife you shall be. He will know how to tame you, and make you docile. You will fawn on the hand you now slight."

"I will never be other than a servant."

"Do you defy my son?"

"I do."

"You!" The woman broke into a discordant laugh. "You! You defy him! A weak girl just out of the nursery, and wont to play with dolls! He has strong hands and iron nerves."

"And I have a strong will, and a resolve of steel."

"He has the force and determination of a lion."

"A lion sleeps!"

"What of that?"

"And a sleeping lion is in the power of a child."

The old mother stepped back, and looked with startled and contracted eyes at the cold, pale girl.

"His wife I shall never be. I will cook for you, scour for you, do what you will about the house, and so earn the meat for my mouth. But let him attempt to urge me, seek to kiss me, let him even venture to address me as his wife, and the county of Shropshire may seek itself another hangman."

"What mean you?"

"I will kill him."

The old woman uttered another of her harsh laughs. Her eyes seemed to draw closer to her nose, as she riveted them with intenser stare on the defiant girl. "Prithee, vixen, how wilt thou accomplish this notable feat?"

"He will be in my power when he is asleep," said Bladys. "Jael, the wife of Heber, drove a nail into the temple of Sisera as he slept, and the prophetess said, 'Blessed be thou among women' for so doing."

"There are no hammer and nails here."

"I need them not."

Bladys put her hand to her hair, and drew forth a long steel pin. "If this were to be thrust into his eye with good resolve, it would penetrate to his brain. He would turn on his bed, cry out, and be dead as Sisera."

Mrs Onion could not speak for a moment. Her blood turned to venom. Her great mouth worked as though she were eating.

After a long pause she said:

"Do you know what is done to the murderess of her husband?"

"I do know."

"Come now, follow me a little way."

Mrs Onion led her from the room along a stone corridor in the thickness of the city wall, lighted only by slots through which the moon gleamed cold on the stone pavement.

"Hark! Hold your breath and listen."

Along the passage came a sobbing, intermittent succession of sounds, now rising into a shriek, then dying away in moans, then broken in spasmodic wails.

"Dost hear that?" asked the old woman. "It is the cry of her who is to die to-morrow. Now I warrant she wishes she had let the old man live, and not lusted to be free to follow the young lover. She thinks of the fire that will consume her on the morrow."

"I will gladly welcome the flames. I will let them embrace me—but never suffer the arms of the hangman to encircle me."

"You shall be watched night and day. I shall not close an eye."

"You cannot always remain waking."

"Then Abraham Jarrock will take my place."

"Abraham Jarrock will look another way whilst I help him to the place of master out of that of assistant."

"You are a devil."

"I was an angel before I was married."

"Your pins and needles shall be taken from you."

They had returned to the illuminated chamber, and Mrs Onion had shut the door.

"I have sharp scissors."

"They also shall be removed."

"I have but to snatch a log from the fire and cast the red ashes about—the old boards are snuff dry, and the Gate House will be in flames and consume you and your son."

"That you cannot do, for you shall not be left alone to work mischief. I shall ever be with you by day, and at night you shall be behind bolt and lock."

"There are other means," said Bladys. "Means that I have learned from a wise woman. I have not been with her in vain."

She drew from her bosom a small packet in coarse brown paper, and from it threw out some ash grey dust on the tablecloth.

"This," said she, "this is Drie. A little sprinkled over the bread, mingled with the pepper, put with the evening caudle, along with the nutmeg, and it will free me from whomsoever I desire to be free."

"Hark!" gasped Mrs Onion. "I hear Luke's hand on the door, his step on the stair. If you will, for the time take yonder chamber. It is over the gate. A servant had it, but she is gone."

"Is there a bolt within?"

"There is a bolt within and a lock without."

"Good, I will take that room."

The old woman thrust the girl through the doorway into the chamber mentioned and indicated.

Bladys at once fastened the door on the inside. Then Mrs Onion turned the key in the lock.

When she had done this she caught up the candle, ran out on the stone landing, and closed the door behind her through which she had just passed.

"Mother," asked Luke Francis, "has she arrived?"

"Yes, someone has come—"

"From Kinver?"

"Yes, from Kinver."

"Let me pass to embrace her."

The old woman stood in the way. Her son looked at her with surprise.

"How your hand shakes," said he. "You are spilling the tallow over your dress, and over the floor. It is running over your hand."

"You cannot go in yet."

"Wherefore not? How your mouth works, mother! What ails thee? What is amiss?"

"Everything."

"With her."

"Ay, with her. Do you know what you have brought to the Gate House?"

"Ay, I trust I do."

"No, you do not, Luke. She is not a wench, she is a white devil."

CHAPTER XII. — PETTY TREASON

On the following morning, at a very early hour, Mrs Onion unlocked the door into the room of Bladys, and knocked sharply. The girl immediately withdrew the bolt and opened.

"Are you in the same mood as last night?" asked the hangman's mother. "Perchance, then, with the journey you were off your reason."

"I am of the same purpose."

"Then," said the old woman, drawing her thin lips against her teeth, "when I give you a command you will obey. Had you said, 'I am Luke's wife,' then I would have answered, 'You are fatigued with travelling; take your ease and repose this day through.' But as it pleases you to be so humorous, then I must lay on you my injunction and expect you to do as I bid. Therefore I say it is my pleasure that you attend me."

"I follow," said Bladys. "Whither?"

"To the Castle. The Foregate is connected with the Castle by a passage in the wall that I showed you overnight."

"I follow and obey."

Thereupon the executioner's mother stepped forward and Bladys followed after her dutifully.

The old woman led along the corridor of stone, stone-paved, and ascending by steps. She mounted a stair of stone, thrust open a door and entered a vaulted chamber in which stood the gaoler and his assistant, as though awaiting her. The former was shaking a bunch of keys, impatient at being delayed.

"She is less troublesome now—that is to say, she is less vociferous in her cries," said the gaoler. "She has made a prodigious noise all through the night. Nothing of that disturbs my sleep, but the other prisoners complained. I have told them that she is to be removed at nine o'clock, and they are vastly satisfied to learn it."

"Open the door," said the old mother.

The turnkey did as he was required, and both were admitted to the cell.

Mrs Onion looked round. There was not much light entering through the small window high up, and which looked north.

"She is gone from here. I do not see her!"

"Oh, she is yonder, assuredly enough. The creature is crouched between the bed and the wall, in the corner. She thinks, poor fool, that she can hide herself and that we shall overlook her."

Then kneeling on the bed, he plucked away the coverlet which the woman had drawn over herself, when she had jammed herself into the cranny where she hoped to find concealment. He laid his hand on her shoulder, not unkindly, and remonstrated with her.

"Now, mistress, this is rank folly! Come forth as a reasonable creature, and do not hug yourself with such notions as that you can escape."

The miserable woman was frantic with terror. Her hair, that was naturally a rich and lustrous chestnut, had fallen about her face and shoulders, and was tangled, sodden, and had lost all its gloss.

"Come now," said the gaoler, "forth from this. You are behaving as a witless child. Pluck up a little courage, and, as a brave woman, face what has to be encountered."

Then she burst into a succession of shrieks.

"I will not die! I cannot die! I am young. I have but twenty-one years. I have but just begun to taste the pleasures of life. I will not die! You shall tear me limb from limb before I am drawn from this place. And to burn! To burn! To burn!" She thrust her fingers through her hair, then cast herself down on the pavement, and scrambled under the bed, with her face to the floor.

"Help me to remove the pallet," said the turnkey. "She has but a mean spirit. A gentlewoman should show more. She should blush to be such a coward."

"Come forth!" ordered Mrs Onion. "You are crushing your gown, and it takes half the worth out of it. It is appointed to all to die, to some early, to others late."

With much difficulty the assistant and his master drew the wretched creature forth, and brought her into the midst of the cell. She would not, or could not, stand.

Her face was soiled with tears, and the stain of a carnation ribbon had come off upon her wet fingers, and had been smeared on her cheeks, that were themselves flaming with the fever that possessed her, flared in her eyes, and distracted her brain.

"I cannot endure fire!" she pleaded in a broken voice between sobs; "look at my finger. I have burnt it—but a small place. I held it to the lamp to feel what fire was. I could not bear it for a second. It made me mad. It was but a little place; it has not raised a blister. How then can I endure that my whole body should burn?"

She gasped, turned her face about, sharply looking from one to the other eagerly, for a token of reprieve. Her breath was hot as fire.

"It will begin at the soles of my feet; there, there, worst of all! And then if a flame springs up to my eyes! They will bind my hands that I cannot hold them up to save my face."

"See this now," said the executioner's mother; "you conceive of matters far worse than they really are. There is, indeed, no requirement that one who is sentenced for petty treason shall not really burn alive, but we are God-fearing and kind-hearted people, and my son is ready to strangle you before the fire takes hold on your body."

"He will strangle me! How—when—with what?"

"Be cheerful, and do not be alarmed without cause. He will loop a stout twine round your throat and the stake. Then with a bit of stick he will give a twist. He has a strong hand, and all will be over. There was a case a few years ago when the executioner failed to do this in time, and recoiled before the flames, so that the woman was burnt alive and was long a-dying. But he was a sad blunderer. My son is not like that. He never fails to do a good deed promptly and right thoroughly."

Then the unhappy prisoner shrieked: "I will not be throttled with a string! I love my life. Life is sweet—it is sweet—and death is more bitter than wormwood."

She covered her heated face and swung from side to side, moaning, the gaoler and his assistant holding her, one on each side.

"Why did my mother force me to marry? I did not know him. I could not care for him. I had no wish to be a wife, but she drove me to it; she tortured me into it. Why do they not burn my mother instead of me? It was her doing. I would never have done him any harm, but that they forced me to be his wife. Why did he take me when he knew that I loved Paul? My mother knew it. He was told it. I swear that I did not mean to kill him. I swear that I purposed only to make him sleep whilst I went away with Paul. I did not know that nightshade would kill him; I thought it would make him sleepy. They will let me off when they know that. I did not have a fair trial. I was not told what was against me. I ask to be tried again. I am unjustly condemned. I will not die! No, I will not die!"*

[* At the date of this story, and indeed long afterwards, prisoners (except in cases of high treason and misdemeanour) could not be defended by counsel. A prisoner had no right to be present at the preliminary investigation before a justice, and the depositions against him were not allowed to be seen, so that the accused should have no opportunity of seeing them. Petty treason is defined as that "when a servant slayeth his master, or a wife her husband, or when a man secular or religious slayeth his prelate to whom he oweth faith and obedience." (25 Ed. III., St. 5, c. 2, A.D. 1352.) In the 75th Chapter of the laws of Henry I. it was punished by flaying alive. The sentence of burning passed on women was not abolished till 1790, when it was changed to drawing and hanging for women, and drawing and burning for men.]

She started to her feet, by a sudden, convulsive effort released herself, and ran round the room, beating the walls with her hands; then she made a rush at the door, but was intercepted by the under-gaoler.

"Let me out!" she cried. "I will go to the judge, and tell him it was a mistake. I did not purpose to kill him. It is he that commits murder when he sentences me to death."

Again she fell into a paroxysm of grief.

Then Mrs Onion said to Bladys, "Lay hold on her, and force her to be seated on the bed."

The girl obeyed. The power to resist further had left the prisoner after her last desperate effort to escape. Assisted by the turnkey, the girl succeeded in controlling her. She took hold of both her wrists.

"Hearken quietly to me," said Mrs Onion. "I have seen many women suffer, but none have cut so poor a figure as yourself. In one half-hour you must be conveyed through the streets. If you have any sense of decency you will be ashamed to be seen as you are, with bedabbled face, stained cheeks, and tangled hair. A woman desires to look her best, even when going to her death. You are a gentlewoman, and should set an example. As a person of fashion you should not appear in this disordered state. Moreover, consider that every woman would wish to awaken regard, pity. Such as you are now, you will provoke none; people will protest, 'She is grumpish, and the world is well rid of such baggage—let her burn.' But if you will permit me to comb your hair, to wash your face, and to take off this habit, that is altogether too smart and unsuitable, and draw over you one of plain serge that is more seemly,—then it will wear another aspect. Folk will look at you with approval, and mark that you are young and pretty, and say that it is a prodigious pity that you were not also honest."

"I cannot—I will not be burned!"

"That gown," said Mrs Onion, "is far too good to be thrust into the fire. Waste is sinful, and you cannot go before your Maker with a fresh crime on your soul. Moreover, it is my perquisite."

"I do not heed my gown. It is I—I—this tender flesh of mine. See how thin the skin is on my throat. I cannot endure it. I feel the smallest prick of a pin!"

Then someone rapped at the cell door. The gaoler opened, and the chaplain appeared.

"My poor woman," said he, "I have come to direct your mind to things above."

"I will not be burnt!" shrieked the woman. "And they threaten to throttle me. I will not be throttled and I will not be burnt. Why is Paul not here? Why has he done nothing to deliver me? Why should I die and not he?"

Then the tears streamed over her cheeks, and being unable to wipe her eyes with her hands, she thrust her wet face against the bosom of Bladys.

Thereupon said Mrs Onion to the chaplain.

"I must ask you, reverend sir, to withdraw a little while—we have to unclothe her and re-cover her with a properer garment. We must wash her face and turn up her hair."

Again the poor creature screamed and battled.

Mrs Onion lost patience.

"This passes all reason. Time is hastening on. Listen! Do you not hear? There is the bell of St Mary's. There are people coming from all quarters, and the execution cannot be stayed to please your humours."

The tolling of the great bell was audible above the hum of voices of people crowding the street.

Awed by the sound, the solemn tone of the bell calling to prayers for the soul of a dying woman, the poor creature desisted from her fruitless efforts, and fell into a sullen lethargy; yet for how long this would last there was no saying. Therefore Mrs Onion hastened to divest her of the gown she wore, and to invest her in an ill-fitting, shabby, darned dress that was of no value.

That accomplished, the chaplain was called in, and the rest withdrew.

When the executioner's mother and Bladys were alone in the stone passage, then the old woman turned to her young companion, and said with a sneer:

"Now you know what it is to commit petty treason. It is no play. Now you have seen what is the agony of the expectation of death. You shall see further the agony of death itself. What think you of petty treason?"

"I think, nay, I am confident," answered Bladys, "that I would gaily endure the same condemnation, rather than be your son's wife. Woe betide him if he venture to forget that I am a servant and no wife." She smiled a frozen smile. "How like you this gown? Passingly? It is the best that I have. It is that wherein I was wed. Do you covet the gown? Then send your son Luke to kiss me, and it is yours by the same title as that you now carry on your arm."

CHAPTER XIII. — THE LAST IN ENGLAND

The old woman conveyed the gown she had taken from her who was to be burnt into a closet where she kept a supply of old garments. Whilst she was absent tears streamed over the pale cheeks of Bladys and a shudder ran through her frame. But by the time Mrs Onion had disposed of the spoil, and was able to return to her, all traces of emotion were past; she was self-possessed as before.

"The cart is already at the Gate, and we must attend her," said the executioner's mother. "I doubt not that we shall have trouble with the creature."

An appealing look from the poor woman, and a clasp of the hand had been given to Bladys, and had been answered by her. Instinct and not reason had told the condemned murderess that there was one heart present that pitied her, that bled for her.

The paroxysms of terror and struggle to be free were past; she had subsided into a condition of stupefaction as the dreaded moment arrived. Despair, like a sudden frost, had enchained all her faculties. She suffered herself to be partly led, partly carried, from the cell, through the Castle yard and gate, and to be lifted into the cart that was to convey her to the spot where she was to die.

Manacles were about her wrists, and an end of the chain attached to them was fastened to a portion of the side of the tumbril. It was deemed advisable to secure her, against another outbreak of frenzied effort to escape.

On her way down the stair of the Castle the unhappy woman held the hand of Bladys. She would not let it go. When it became necessary, at the moment of her being placed in the conveyance, to disengage her hold, she became restive and stretched her arms beseechingly towards Bladys; and yet, not a word had passed between them, and till that morning neither had seen the other.

The chaplain walked by the side of the tumbril, addressing exhortations as best he could; but few of his words were audible, owing to the rattle of the wheels over the pavement, the effervescence of the crowd, and strangely incongruous—the drone of a hurdy-gurdy. The Savoyard had come to Shrewsbury, and regardless of everything else, sought to gain a few coppers by the exhibition of his dancing ape. His efforts to attract attention were in vain, the crowd had other and more interesting matters to engage their eyes and thoughts.

The tumbril was guarded by the javelin men of the Sheriff who himself followed in his coach. The miserable woman looked with staring, wild eyes from side to side, and then into the face of Bladys, who sat beside her in the straw. Then, drawing herself up so as to speak in her ear, and to be heard above the noise, she said:

"There will be a reprieve—a pardon. Tell me there will. They will not really burn me."

The hum of the populace was like the mutter of the sea after a storm, when the rollers come in on the beach, but without a wind to propel them. The hurdy-gurdy was no longer audible. It had been left behind. St Mary's bell boomed, sending throbs of sound overhead that beat against the walls of the house in one street, and came back muffled in recoil.

The street was thronged with people. Some houses had the blinds drawn down and doors shut, and no signs of inhabitants showing. Others had windows, doors, parapet crowded with people. Some lookers-on had awe-stricken faces; others exhibited only curiosity. Few, apparently, had any sympathy with the woman who had been untrue to her husband, and had compassed his death, but some felt that the mode of execution was barbarous. Already at the close of the eighteenth century the notion had begun to be entertained that the punishment inflicted by the law was cruel and disproportionate to the offence, and this feeling manifested itself intermittently where were drawn blinds and closed shops.

Eyes were directed upon Bladys, as well as on the condemned woman. Some asked, "Who is that young female in the cart?"

To which answer was made, "We have been informed that the hangman has been outside of the county to get himself a wife."

"Ah!" the querists would throw in, "he must needs go where he is unknown, for no girl would have him who was aware of his trade."

Then another would remark, "Anyhow, she takes vastly kindly to the business."

"Not so. See how pale she is. Od's life, she might be going herself to execution."

The tumbril arrived at the descent towards the Severn, and those seated in it could see the narrow street, winding among black-timbered and plastered houses, packed with people and the javelin men thrusting and pushing their way with difficulty, so as to effect a clearance and open a road for the cart.

The woman on her way to death was shivering, as though with frost in the marrow of her bones, and her teeth chattered. Turning a ghastly face on Bladys, she stammered, "There is the bridge; there is the—" and with a shriek she threw herself upon the girl who was sitting with her. "Save me! save me! and I will give you something worth your pains. I will give it you; it shall be all your own."

The cry of the woman had produced a sudden lull in the voices. They sank into stillness, only broken by the boom of the bell and the clatter of the wheels over the cobblestones. Now, also, the voice of the chaplain rose, as he recited a penitential psalm: "Wash me throughly from my wickedness, and cleanse me from my sin. For I acknowledge my faults, and my sin is ever before me!" When the procession attained the bridge, then the poor woman looked towards the water, and made a spasmodic effort to free herself, with a half-articulate desire in her troubled mind to throw herself into the river. A death by drowning were preferable to that in store for her. But there were boats on the water, and men in the boats, stretching their necks to have a sight of the convoy. Had she cast herself in, she would have at once been fished out; moreover, she had been fastened to the cart by the executioner, who had foreseen some such attempt.

Now there went by a rush of swifts screaming, pursuing one that had robbed a nest, or had been faithless to her spouse. The bird that was chased turned in the air and did battle with its pursuers, and the posse of swifts, regardless of the human crowd below, dashed hither and thither, but a little way above their heads, making a loud and angry din, plucking out feathers from the bird they had combined to punish, and attentive to their own concerns and the execution of their own judgment only.

In front rose the magnificent, half-ruined minster; in our own days nobly restored, to be one of the grandest churches in England. Hard by—among the fragments of the conventual buildings—stands a solitary pulpit of stone, of exquisite design. This was now occupied by a strange figure; it was that of an old man in a patched coat, with a rolling collar and a white cravat. He was gesticulating and declaiming. This man was, in fact, Holy Austin, who had come from Kinver, moved by inner wrath and zeal against injustice in the execution of justice, seizing occasion to address the crowd.

A ring of people had formed round the pulpit, and listened with signs of impatience to him, enduring his diversion of their attention with as little tolerance as a similar crowd near the Castle had shown to the Savoyard and his hurdy-gurdy. Now, as then, the appearance of the principal personage in the tragedy drew away attention at once. Those who had been facing the orator with one accord turned their backs and made a rush to secure good positions near the stake. Rough men, laughing, swearing, scrambled up the pulpit, as the steps were blocked, thrust the speaker into the rear, and appropriated to themselves the positions which commanded the stake. The circle of constables surrounding the place of execution opened to allow the cart to pass within, and in so doing disclosed the pile of faggots, and the post rising above it, to which was attached a hoop that was to clasp the waist of the victim and prevent her from sinking in shame and anguish into the element that surged up from below.

A fire burning in an extemporised grate of iron bars and bricks near the ground, composed of dry wood, blazed merrily, throwing up spirals of flame and a light, pungent smoke. The purpose was obvious enough. At this grate were to be kindled the brands by means of which the pyre was to be lighted simultaneously in three places.

The poor victim, on seeing the flames and smelling the reek which blew in her face, became again desperate, and writhed with such force that it required four men to restrain her.

Her cries, and the sight of the struggle, sent a thrill of terrible ecstasy through the spectators. Even the most callous shuddered. Some turned sick and faint, and elbowed their way out of the crowd, unable to endure more.

When the unhappy creature became visible, in the arms of the executioners, who were by main force lifting her upon the pyre, and when they saw the hoop being riveted about her, then all who witnessed the proceedings uttered a gasp. Those who could see nothing made frantic efforts to elevate themselves by leaping, standing on tiptoe, or grappling such as were taller than themselves. One fond father lifted his little child to his shoulder and believed he was giving him a fine moral object-lesson.

And now the hangman slipped a cord about the neck of the condemned woman and passed it round the stake. She endeavoured to get at it with her hands, but they were fastened behind her back, then to bite it asunder with her teeth, to slip her head under it—any way to free herself from the stricture that was destined to throttle the life out of her.

She gasped, "Stay! stay! I see someone waving his hand. He bears a pardon."

But the executioner's mother answered, "That is but a preacher who is exhorting the people and bidding them take warning by your fate."

"There is a man getting out of a coach. He bears a reprieve."

"That is the sheriff, who comes to see that the sentence of the law be duly carried out."

"Hush! I hear a voice crying! He is declaring that I am to go free."

"That is the chaplain reading the burial service." And the priest's solemn tones rose in her ear:

"In the midst of life we are in death. Of whom may we seek for succour, but of Thee, O Lord, who for our sins are justly displeased."

"One moment! One moment more! Let me say a word to her."

She signed with her head to Bladys. Then the latter stepped upon the pile of faggots and drew close to the poor woman. She, with ashen face, leaden lips, and starting eyes, turned to her and said, "I have no hope now. It is nearly over. Put your hand into my bosom. They did not find it when they stripped me of my gown. It is for you."

"What is it?"

"What I spoke of before. It is for you only. I cannot die with the secret, and leave it to any one who may chance to find it. You alone have had compassion. You alone pity me. I have none else to think for, to care about. It is for you."

Then Bladys thrust her hand where desired and drew forth a small packet.

"Put it away," sobbed the unhappy woman. "Let none else see it. Let none else have it or any share of it. It is all for you." She panted. Then in a hoarse voice said, "Wipe my face."

With her handkerchief Bladys dried the tears, the sweat of mortal anguish which bathed the livid face.

And that whole vast concourse of sightseers kept silence. There was absolute stillness.

The executioner who stood behind the stake had his hand on the tourniquet and delayed. But there was a glitter in his eye, and he signed to the girl with a movement of his head. Then it was that—moved by intense pity—Bladys kissed the poor victim on the cheek. Instantly a mighty roar, like the bursting of a dam, the invasion of a flood.

Next moment Bladys was snatched from the pyre, plucked down, and thrust back.

Still the roar continued, it swelled in volume, it grew to an ominous thunder. It spurted into articulate cries of "Stone him! Cast him into the fire! Smash the sheriff's carriage! Save her! It is not yet too late."

But it was too late! The woman was dead.

What the people were about was this:—That kiss given by Bladys to her that was condemned to a horrible death was seen by the vast concourse; and that sight had wrought an effect extraordinary, incredible, revolutionary.

Instantaneously it had unlocked and set free all the humanity that had been sealed up in ten thousand hearts. It had struck a film from the eyes of every man and woman present, and they saw plainly, for the first time in their lives, that this execution, with its publicity, its barbarity, was a worse crime than that committed by the woman under sentence.

That pitiful kiss given on the pyre—given in welling-over human love to the poor, broken victim—had let loose the Christian compassion that had been in a death-trance for more than seventeen hundred years.

It had been proclaimed as a Divine law by Him who stooped and wrote in the dust, when the sinful woman was brought before Him by her judges. Christian prelates had not felt it stirring when they sent heretics to the stake, nor Christian kings when they had condemned traitors to be drawn and quartered, nor Christian legislators when they adjudicated to the gallows the man who stole a sheep, and the maid who purloined half-a-crown. The excitement, the emotion roused by the kiss of Bladys, as is so generally the case with an unthinking crowd, took a wrong direction. In an explosion of resentment, it vented itself against the hangman who had strangled the woman, against his assistants for igniting the pyre, against the sheriff who had conducted the execution, against the constables who had endeavoured to keep order. But there was more than a roar of human voices. Waves of human beings swayed to and fro actuated by one passion of indignation. They sent up a foam of brandished sticks and hands in agitation, casting stones. There were seen men flying, wands wavering; there were heard cries from such as fell and were trampled on, or were thrust against the blazing pile, and were singed, by such as trod in the oozing tar, or stumbled over the preparatory fire, or were jammed between the wheels of the sheriff's carriage. Yet above all rang the shrill cry of Holy Austin from the stone pulpit.

"My brothers, you do wrong. It is not the hangman who is in fault; he but fulfils the duty for which he is paid. Nor is the sheriff to blame; he sees to the execution of the laws. It is with the inhuman criminal laws of England that the sin lies. They are a disgrace to a Christian land; they are a stain on modern civilisation. You have votes; you send your deputies to Parliament. Unite and insist on this—that such barbarous enactments be swept away."

The kiss of Bladys and the words of Austin were not lost. They did not arouse the multitude, and give direction to their indignation, in vain. They produced their effect beyond Shrewsbury. They had a far more extended effect.

In the same year, 1790, that this poor woman was burnt at Shrewsbury, in the very next session of Parliament, this method of execution was abolished, and the crime of petty treason was struck out of the Statutes.

CHAPTER XIV. — A CHALLENGE

A mob in ebullition, traversed by currents in various directions—such was the scene presented by the open space before the west front of the Abbey Church.

One stream set towards the stake, where hung the strangled woman in the midst of rising smoke and lambent flames. Another drove in pursuit of the flying executioner and his assistants. A third made for the bridge, to escape into the town from a tumult in which blood might, and probably would, be shed, and which would entail an unpleasant after-reckoning.

A stone had broken a window of the sheriff's carriage, but he had let down the glass, projected his head, and was haranguing, threatening the mob, and was calling on his javelin men to rally around him. These, however, had been dispersed and no longer formed a homogeneous body, and having lost cohesion, had lost with it all the little courage they possessed.

On the bridge was a jam, caused by a horseman endeavouring to make way through the mass of human beings encumbering it and constricted between the parapets. He had been despatched to invoke the aid of the military.

The wind was from the east, and it drove the smoke over the bridge, sickly with the odour of the singed and now burning garments of the dead woman. Some of the rabble insensately began to tear the fire to pieces, as though that would avail the poor creature. She was, in fact, dead before the flame had leaped up and licked her face and curled around her bowed frame. The attempts made to level the pyre only served to scatter the blazing faggots, endangering those who stood near, and such as were thrust into dangerous proximity by the press of the crowd.

The javelin men, dispersed, were spun like teetotums in the swirl, and gradually concentrated around the sheriff's carriage, although when there too frightened to attend to his instructions, and too powerless to execute them.

Mother Onion had clutched the wrist of Bladys, and now dragged her towards the bridge. She had snatched the shawl from the latter, and had thrown it over her own head with the object of concealing her features.

"They know me. They are angry with us all. They are mad, and might injure me. You they do not know, and against you they bear no grudge. Come! Be quick! I pray God no harm has befallen my son. The people have lost their wits. It is all your doing. Why did you kiss her? Before that they were prepared to relish the execution, as they have done heretofore. Keep near me. Conceal me with your person as best you may. What was that you took from her? Was it gold? She was rich. Do not lag thus. We must press on; I am not safe. We must get home at greatest speed. Od's-zounds! If they were to recognise me, there is no telling, in their present humour, but they might cast me into the flames."

As the old woman, grappling Bladys, worked her way over the bridge, she rang changes on her alarm for herself, concern for her son, and impatience to learn what that was which Bladys had taken at the last moment from the woman on the pyre.

The stream set strongly across the bridge, but near the middle was brought to a standstill by the rider, as already mentioned; and then the old woman was driven against the parapet and nearly thrown down.

The pressure was relieved when the messenger had passed, and then the current resumed its flow, now with increased rapidity, and it carried Mother Onion and Bladys into the main street of Shrewsbury, at the place where once stood the Western Gate, which had been demolished before the date of this tale.

"Come aside, along this lane," said the executioner's mother. "We shall stand less chance of being observed. I trust in Heaven that no ill has come upon Luke. He was discharging his duty. He was acting the good Samaritan. The law requires that the woman sentenced for petty treason shall be burnt alive, but my son, as a humane man, and one that fears God, and loves his neighbour, mitigates the penalty. He is not required to do so. He does it because he has a good heart, and those sentenced usually pay handsomely to be spared the greater pain of burning. Why, then, should the people be incensed against him? What did you take from her? I obtained nothing but an old gown that will not fetch a guinea. She had none of her rings on her fingers, not even the wedding ring. They belong to me by rights. Nicodemus, the gaoler, has no wife, and I attend to the criminals. He is avaricious. Do you think he removed the rings before I was called in? Or had she concealed them in her bosom, and did she give them to you?"

Bladys made no reply.

As there was now no crush, and the lateral alley was clear of the crowd, the old woman halted, and, tugging at her daughter-in-law's wrist, said, impatiently, "I must be told. What did you get from her?"

"I do not know," answered Bladys coldly.

"But, look you, I must learn. She was rich. She had gold. She was a jeweller's daughter."

"I took from her a small package, but I have not examined nor have I opened it. Let that suffice."

"It shall not suffice. I must see the contents."

"Whatever the contents may be they are not for you."

"That's purely! Not for me! And mayhap there may be a hundred guineas."

"I do not think that it contains money. Mayhap it is but a commission; perhaps a lock of hair; perhaps a message of love; perhaps a confession of guilt. I have not looked, and I shall not look till I am alone in my chamber with the door locked against intrusion."

"Lack-a-day! A saucy minx! But I shall insist on having a sight too; and if you refuse Luke shall help me to it presently."

"Whatever it is," replied Bladys, in a dispassionate tone, "it is not for you. She said to me, 'Take it; I give it to you alone. You only have shown me kindness.' Whether it be a trust or a bequest—whatever it be—it is to me sacred from prying eyes and impertinent curiosity."

"Hey-day!" The old woman was convulsed with rage. "Is this the manner in which you address me? Impertinent curiosity, quotha! I warrant you, it is a hundred guineas. That is Luke's fee. He has not been paid for what he did—for strangling her instead of suffering her to burn alive. It is his due. She promised it to him."

"I do not believe you. She made no such promise. But to set your mind at rest," the girl put her hand to her bosom, "the parcel has no such a feeling as if it contained gold."

"There may be notes."

"It feels to me as though it contained a letter, and therewith a small key."

"A key! Let me read the letter. A key to what?"

"That in no way concerns you."

"I will know."

Bladys turned herself about, looked the woman in the face, and answered:

"My will is stronger than yours."

"We shall see."

Nothing further was said till the Gate House was reached, and then Mrs Onion ascended the stairs before Bladys. At the landing she turned her head over her shoulder and said:

"Are you his servant or his wife?"

"I have already informed you."

"Then," exclaimed the old woman, with a fierce leap in her manner, "give up the package. As his wife you would have a right to it; for it belongs to the executioner by customary right to have whatever the criminal wears or carries about him or her at execution; but if you are a servant, what you have and retain is stolen—it is a theft, for which you can be charged. I pray to Heaven you may not come to pass through Luke's hands to the gallows!"

"I will bear the risk."

Then Mrs Onion opened the door of the kitchen. Changing her tone, she said:

"It is our custom, after an execution, that the gaoler or the hangman, one or the other, gives a supper to all who were engaged. It is not this time the turn of Nicodemus. It falls to Luke." With a sneer, she added: "Your master if you will. I pray the Lord that my son is safe. If he has come to harm, it is your doing. Wherefore did you kiss that sinful woman, and so rouse the mob upon us? Did you reckon they would fall on Luke and tear him to pieces, and so set you free from him?"

She looked about her and muttered. Presently she proceeded:

"There are three turnkeys and Abraham Jarrock, Ap Rice, and my son Luke. I have a round of beef ready, but there are other things to be prepared. I count on you."

"I will help," answered Bladys

An hour later Abraham arrived out of breath and surly. He was eagerly questioned by Mrs Onion.

"The master has had his scalp cut open by a stick, but the skull is not broken. We slipped away, he and I. What became of Ap Rice I know not. Luke and I went into the Abbey Church, and fast barred the door behind us. The parson was within, and he assisted us. The fellows without hammered at one door and then at another, trying to get at us. God knows what they would have done had they reached us. One man was shouting 'Hang them to the bell-ropes!' At last the vicar smuggled us out by a small door at the east end, and you'd have laughed, for Luke wore his cassock and looked like a parson. The vicar lent him his wig to cover his cut scalp. He was taken to Surgeon Bett's to have his head sewn up. No harm done. There he abides till night falls and he can return without risk."

"Do you think," said Mrs Onion, "that Luke will have stomach for his meat?"

"Will he not! This is not only the gallows supper, but his wedding feast."

"His wedding feast!" echoed the old woman.

"Well, my pretty mistress," said the assistant, turning to Bladys, "how goes the honeymoon? Sweet, eh?"

"Sweet!" repeated Mrs Onion, and her bile overflowed. "What think you to this, Abraham? She denies that she is his wife. She threatens that she will burn down the Gate House if he do but touch her. Is it not so?"

Mrs Onion turned to Bladys, her eyes contracting with malice. The girl replied with coolness, "I said as much."

"And further, she protests that she will poison him—as did that woman we burned to-day."

"Anything rather than be his wife," said Bladys.

"That is not all," pursued the hangman's mother. "She threatens that when he sleeps she will drive her hairpin into his brain."

Then Abraham Jarrock set his hands to his side and broke into loud laughter.

"Dost count it a jest?" asked Mrs Onion angrily, "that he has brought such a woman into this house?"

"I do laugh," answered Jarrock. "Be without concern. Madam, a woman who brags—that is not the woman who will do the deed. Pshaw! The doers are not the talkers."

When darkness had settled in, Luke Onion arrived. His cut scalp had been patched, he was haggard, and in evil mood, answering his mother's questions churlishly, and manifesting impatience at her expressions of sympathy. He looked out of the corners of his eyes at Bladys, to observe whether she was disposed to pity him in his battered condition, but she vouchsafed him neither look nor word.

"Is the riot at an end?" asked Mrs Onion.

"The riot, ay! The disturbance not. The streets are full of people, and the constables have been arresting, of course, the wrong folk, letting the ringleaders run free."

"Luke," said his mother, "dost know how and by whom this riot was stirred up?"

As her son made no reply, she went on—

"It was all her doing—she who has been a trouble since she entered this house. It was she who stirred up the people against you. It is to her you owe the shame, the disgrace of this day. It is to her you are indebted for your cut head. And she has thieved as well. She has taken from us that which is ours and not hers. Come, Luke, we have had nought but unpleasantness since she entered the house. Let her surrender what she took from the woman, and after that cast her out of the house."

"Let her go?" laughed Luke sardonically. "Not I, indeed. That would be rare jest—that I should be robbed of my money and wife together."

"She has taken gold of the woman."

"Whatever I received," said Bladys, "that I retain. I have had time to look at what she gave me. Be assured, there is neither gold nor jewel therein, only a scribble of a few words."

"What words."

"They are for me alone."

"You said there was a key."

"Yes; a small key."

"To what?"

"I cannot tell."

"Now, hark you," said Luke Onion. "Petty treason involves forfeiture. If there be gold I take it as my fee—you cannot retain it"

"There was, as I said, no gold."

"Luke, send her away."

"Mother, set your mind at ease. She does not escape me. I am not one to be opposed or frightened by a woman. As to threats, I laugh at them."

Then swinging himself about, he gripped Bladys with both hands, holding her head as in a vice, and looking straight into her eyes, he said:

"Do you still defy me, hussy?"

"Still."

"Is it to be a struggle between us until one buckles under?"

"Or dies!"

"Or dies. Very well. I accept the challenge."

The day of an execution was one that gave satisfaction alike to turnkey, hangman, and their assistants, for it was to them the conclusion of a harvest reaped out of the unfortunate who had fallen into their hands, and in the evening it was customary with them to make merry over the plunder and to keep their harvest home.

No sooner was a prisoner sent to the Castle than a system of pillage began, to which he and his relatives were subjected, and which did not cease till he was discharged or executed.

Within the gaol, his comforts, almost his necessaries of life, had to be bought of the head turnkey. A poor prisoner fared badly. He had a miserable cell, where he was abandoned to filth and famine. The discomforts of a recalcitrant prisoner were rendered daily more acute till his resistance was broken, and he submitted to the exactions of those who held him in control; till he allowed himself as a human wreck to be boarded and pillaged until nothing was left on him that was worth taking. He had to pay for his food, for his drink, for clean bedding, for fuel, even for privacy. The gaoler was well aware that the most intolerable annoyance to which he could subject those of a better class was to crush them into a common day-room with the worst criminals of the most degraded order, and to associate in one bedroom the most unsuitable companions. Consequently he exacted a heavy fee for the privilege of a separate apartment. Nor was it the gaoler alone that preyed on the victim of Justice, so-called. A criminal condemned to death was at the mercy of the hangman, who was to be bribed to "turn him off" speedily, and who, unless satisfied, might prolong his agony. The woman sentenced to death by fire had to buy the concession of being strangled at the stake; the man who was to be hung purchased with gold every inch of the drop.

Visitors out of curiosity could always buy permission to interview the prisoner; relations—mother, wife, children—could obtain no parting embrace without having fed the gaoler.

The system of flaying was not confined to the period of life; it was continued after death, and that no longer metaphorically. In the case of hanging, the executioner sold the rope at a guinea an inch, and even took the skin off the dead man's back and chest, and vended it in squares as charms that were eagerly purchased by the superstitious. The hangman claimed the clothing of those sentenced to death as a customary perquisite, in addition to the fee paid him by the County for the execution. In the Orient the vultures swoop upon the dead, but in the West, England not excepted, before the improvements due to the exertions of Howard, the prisoner was a prey to human vultures from the moment that he passed through the gates before his trial.

The supper given by Luke Onion and his fellow-vultures on the evening ensuing the execution for petty treason was not lacking in boisterousness, although not wholly as free as on former occasions. The cuts and bruises received by Luke and his assistants somewhat damped their hilarity, and the manifestation of popular indignation had left on them a vague and uneasy suspicion that a revolution in the method of treatment of criminals, and a modification of the barbarity of medieval methods, was not improbable— and any such change would menace their interests.

But although their spirits might have a brush of gloomy forecast, yet this in no way affected their appetite, and least of all their thirst.

They ate ravenously and drank heavily, and were served by Mrs Onion and Bladys.

The pain and agonies of his cut scalp made Luke silent, they gave a feverish glitter to his eye, and brought hot rushes of blood into his cheeks. His hand was unsteady, and he occasionally opened his lips to speak, then checked himself. His silence was observed and interpreted by the guests in their own fashion. Although linked together by common interest, and common resistance to all improvement in the condition of prisons and the treatment of prisoners, yet among themselves existed much jealousy, spite, and rancour.

"How now, Luke Francis?" shouted Nicodemus, the gaoler. "What is the truth in this tale that is in every mouth in Shrewsbury—that you fell among thieves, who despoiled you of your raiment and left you half-dead?"

"And further," cast in Jarrock maliciously, "that they kissed your wife and capered with her on the green, whilst you played the fiddle?"

"A lie!" said the hangman surlily.

"To be sure, it is a lie throughout," said Abraham. "We know the master too well to believe that he would allow himself to be waylaid, and to have his pockets turned inside out by highwaymen."

"I do not deny that footpads stopped the carriage," said Onion, in confusion and anger.

"Nor that you were robbed?" asked Nicodemus.

"Nor that your wife was kissed?" inquired Jarrock.

"The tale I have heard," said the under-gaoler, "is that Mr Onion showed no fight."

"It is true that I was robbed," said Luke, with flaming face. "I was taken by surprise. I was with my wife. I had just left the altar, where we had plighted our vows. Who, under such circumstances, would not be liable to be thrown off his guard?"

"I could not have believed," said Nicodemus, "that Luke Francis Onion, Executioner to the Counties of Shropshire and Staffordshire, should have suffered himself under any circumstances to be stayed by footpads and not fire a pistol or brandish a cutlass in self-defence. You were armed, I doubt not."

"I was caught before I had time to get at my pistols," said the hangman, every muscle in his face and hands working with vexation and shame. "Change the matter; this is distasteful to me."

"Distasteful it may be," pursued the gaoler. "Yet it is one that concerns us all, for ours are sister callings. No marvel if the vulgar mob rose to-day against the ministers of justice who were too pusillanimous to defend themselves against open and notorious breakers of the law."

"By heaven, I swear," roared Onion, "it shall not pass unpunished! Caught I was, and robbed as well; I do not deny it. But I exult in the fact—I exult in it for this reason—that these rascals have delivered themselves into my hands. Rats may eat the meat strewn for them a dozen times with impunity—but the thirteenth time it is mingled with poison. These highwaymen have long been a terror in the land. Hitherto they have baffled pursuit. They have escaped all officers sent to apprehend them; and for a good reason, because none knew who they were, so carefully did they cover their traces, so well-concealed their runs, and so well-chosen their haunts."

"Well, and now?"

"And now I know where to find them, and can put my hand upon their captain."

"You know them?"

"Ay! I know their ringleader, John Poulter, alias Baxter. You have heard of him?"

"Ay! Who has not? What is his real name?"

"I have learned it. I know where he lives. But I should never have discovered either had not my carriage been stayed. Had I not gone down to Kinver parish and tarried a fortnight at the Stewponey, I should not have known."

"Listen to this," jeered Nicodemus. "He sings two strains. First he admits that he was stayed and robbed against his will; now he would have it that the whole was a trap laid by him with vast ingenuity to catch the rats. If you know who the captain is—what's his true name—speak it; and we will believe you."

"I will not tell you," shouted Luke, in a fever of irritability. "I am not singing two strains. The calash was stopped, and we were forced to descend from it. I was plundered, I do not deny that; nor do I assert that it was premeditated and planned by myself. I will add that the Captain danced a measure on the turf with her yonder." He indicated Bladys with his thumb. "An Italian with a hurdy-gurdy was constrained to play a tune. In the moonlight they danced; and as they danced he held up his right hand, thinking to appear graceful in his postures. Then I perceived that his forefinger was crooked, stiffened into a pothook. I knew him by that, immediately; for I had played at bowls on several evenings with one who had such a crooked finger at the Stewponey, and then he had been unmasked. Thus I came to know who he is, and what his right name. When I choose, which shall be soon, I shall have him. All I tarry for is warrants made out in three counties, so that he may not slip away over the border and escape us."

"Is he a gentleman, Luke?"

"Ay, he and the rest."

"Hurrah! mates. There will be meat on his bones!"

Ap Rice, the apprentice, willing to stand well with his master, said:

"Let him laugh who wins. It was worth the loss of a few crowns to be able to take so great a thief."

"He is not yet taken," said Nicodemus.

"He will be by the heels in a week."

"Ah!" said Abraham, who delighted in girding at his superior, "if but a few crowns had been taken, that would have been nothing, it would have been repairable. But it is commonly reported that Captain Poulter robbed the master of something he can never recover, do what he may."

"What may that be?" asked one of the turnkeys.

"If all that is told be true," said Jarrock, with a malicious smile on his lips, "the Captain not only took a kiss from the bride, but stole her heart away as well, and so effectually secured it, that now she will not allow Luke Onion even to look into her eyes, even to wish for a taste of her lips."

"Here comes the punch! the primest pine-apple rum," shouted the hangman, as his mother and Bladys entered, bearing the steaming bowl.

Then one of the gaolers sang:

"Come all you old minstrels, wherever you be.
With comrades united in sweet harmony.
Whilst the clear crystal fountain thro' England shall roll.
Give me the Punch Ladle—I'll fathom the Bowl.
Let nothing but harmony reign in your breast;
Let comrade with comrade be ever at rest.
We'll toss off our bumper, together we'll troll.
Give me the Punch Ladle—I'll fathom the Bowl."

Then Jarrock, with an ugly sneer and a wink, and with finger pointed first to Onion and then to Bladys, sang in a harsh tone—

"Our wives they may bluster as much as they please.
Let 'em scold, let 'em grumble, we'll sit at our ease.
To the ends of our pipes we'll apply a hot coal.
Give me the Punch Ladle—I'll fathom the Bowl."

"Drink the health of the bride!" shouted Nicodemus. "Come, mistress. Take your place at table, and here's to your lord and master. Give the lie to Jarrock's scandal. Here's to the bride!"

"Come on, mistress!" called Abraham. "If you will not sit by Luke, I will make a place for you by myself. We spent some pleasant hours together between Stourton and Shrewsbury."

"Sit down!" shouted all. "Luke, make her honour and obey if she cannot love. Sit down. We are going to toast you."

Then all rose with a roar, and waved their glasses.

Bladys escaped through the doorway, into her room above the gate, and bolted the door.

"Luke Onion, make her come," called Nicodemus. "She don't show you nor us proper respect."

Onion, infuriated by the banter, galled by the words of Jarrock, stung by the slight put upon him by Bladys, leapt to his feet, rushed to the door, and, striking it with his feet and fists, bellowed:

"Come out instantly, I command you!"

All present became silent, holding their punch-glasses in hand, some of which were filled, others extended to be supplied, and looked towards the door expectantly.

No reply was vouchsafed to the command. The bolt was not withdrawn. Again the hangman struck at it, and with an oath called:

"Come forth, or I'll break it open." Still no reply, no movement.

The men at the table tittered, nudged each other, and twinkled their eyes at one another.

The head turnkey said:

"This is very like to that scene in the Scripture, where the King sent for Vashti, and she would not come."

"Ay," said Jarrock, "but when Vashti refused to come, he took another in her room. By Heaven! there is the rub. There be no Esther who will have him. He has been five years questing a Vashti!"

This sally produced a burst of laughter, and roused Luke's anger to madness. He became livid with rage, and, in the excitement, the stitches that closed his wound gave way, and blood trickled down the side of his face. He set his teeth, his eyes glared; he went to an outer chamber, and returned with a crowbar.

With this he smote at the bedroom door.

"Come out," he roared. "I will beat in the panels; I will drag you forth by the hair."

Then he belaboured the door with a fury that gathered at every blow. Splinters came off and flew about the room.

Mother Onion hastened to her son, and endeavoured to pacify him, by representations that the scene was not a seemly one to exhibit before his guests; that she whom he summoned was unworthy of his anger, and was best left to herself. But he would not hearken. His blood was boiling, his brain on fire. He flung himself with his full weight against the oak door; he drove the point of the bar in at the joint, that he might work the hinges out of their sockets in the solid stone into which they were soldered.

Then suddenly the alarm bell that hung above the gate rang out its summons fast and vehement.

Instantly every glass was set down on the table. Onion lowered the bar and fell back. A look of dismay spread over his face.

"She will rouse the town!"

"She will bring the mob on us again!"

"They will murder us all, this time!"

Then Nicodemus, in an agitated voice, said:

"Make her cease. Promise anything."

Luke leaned on his crowbar, panting for breath, his eyes flaring as with summer lightnings.

Then Nicodemus himself went to the door, and called:

"Mrs Onion!"

Still the bell continued to peal.

Jarrock laughed and said:

"She will not respond to that name."

"Then how shall I call her? By—we must stay the bell."

Thereupon Abraham Jarrock took his place against the door and shouted:

"Stewponey Bladys! Name your own terms and you shall go free."

At once the bell ceased, and in the lull that ensued was heard a hubbub of voices without.

"The people are gathering!" whispered Mother Onion.

"They will break in the door!" gasped Ap Rice.

Then Bladys said distinctly in reply:

"Let the head gaoler in the name of all swear to let me depart untouched, not to suffer a finger to be laid upon me."

"I swear!" answered the turnkey.

At once the bolt was withdrawn, the door was thrown open, and Bladys came forth, self-possessed and white as snow.

The men were standing at the table, some with their hands on it. Luke made an attempt to strike at her with the crowbar, but Abraham fell upon him, dashed him against the wall, and wrenched the weapon from his hands.

"You fool!" he said, "will you give the mob an excuse for tearing us to pieces?"

Then Nicodemus stood forward and said;

"Go your way; none shall molest you."

He stepped back to the table, took up his glass, raised it, and said:

"Here is to you! A brave wench! I honour you—but your place is not here. Drink to her, lads."

His command was silently obeyed.

"Now," said he, "Mother Onion, attend her to the door. My lads, let not that mad fellow touch her."

Mrs Onion grasped the shoulder of Bladys and thrust her before her through the doorway and down the stone steps, opened the door of the house, and with a push sent her into the street with such precipitation as would have thrown her to the pavement had she not been caught.

The street was filling. Windows were thrown open and heads appeared at them. Cries were audible— more people were hurrying to the gate in answer to the call of the bell.

"Stewponey Bla!" exclaimed a cheerful voice. Bladys found herself in the arms of Nancy Norris.

CHAPTER XVI. — DRIE

In the obscurity, rendered doubly obscure by contrast with the lighted room she had left, Bladys might not have recognised the person who received her in her arms and with a kiss, but there was no mistaking the fresh voice of Nan.

"So, we have got you!" exclaimed the latter. "We have found out about you. But what is the meaning of that bell? Did you ring it? Folks are running from all the town."

"Yes, Nan, I did sound it."

"What is the matter? Is there a fire anywhere?"

"There is no fire. I rang to oblige them to release me."

"Them! Whom dost mean? Then you are free?"

"Yes, I will never return to them."

"That is brave. Now that we have recovered you, we will carry you away. It was cowardly of the fellow to take you to church and marry you, without letting you know to whom and to what manner of man you were wed."

"Let us go from this place; a crowd is collecting."

"It is so. By Goles! It is you who have summoned it, and they desire to be told what is amiss. That is, they say, the fire-bell; and the people think that some house burns."

There rose on all sides shouts, and a general clamour about the Gate.

The window of the chamber lately occupied by Bladys, that immediately over the gate, was thrown open, and a man appeared at it—Nicodemus, the turnkey.

"Good people of Shrewsbury," he called, "have no further concern. There threatened to be a conflagration here, in the County executioner's apartments, but the danger is past. The fire has been extinguished. Return to your homes."

Then one in the throng shouted:

"If the Gate House had burnt, with the hangman and his dam, and with the rest of you in it, we would have been well rid of the crew."

"Ay," vociferated another, "and not one of us would have put forth a finger to save you."

"Mates," called a third, "what say you? Shall we kindle the fire again, and stir it well, that this time it shall not go out?"

"Where's the good attempting it?" answered another, "when they can escape into the Castle?"

"Here arrive the constables," said another.

"Come from hence," said Nan to Bladys; and linking her arm within that of the girl from Stewponey, she forced a passage through the crowd.

"So you have deserted him. That is as it should be. I'd fancy Abraham before him—and he is currish, and a hangman's assistant, and will be head executioner some day. By Goles! When the gentlemen stayed the carriage on the heath, had they known who was there, they would not have contented themselves with taking his silver and kissing his wife."

"That was not done," interrupted Bladys.

"What odds? They danced with you; and any wench would be proud to be kissed by—by a gentleman of the road, and a captain to boot. But, as I was saying, had they suspected who this Luke Francis was, then, I protest, they would not have suffered him to run, but they would have strung him to the first tree, and let him taste of the medicine he has administered to so many good boys."

Nan continued working her way forward, drawing Bladys along with her.

"What do you think, now? My old mother is in Shrewsbury. She swore she could not die happy without having seen a woman burnt, and she laid it upon George Stracey to take her, as he had planned to drive me up to the execution; and he was good enough to consent to take her also. So we came all three together to Shrewsbury. He drove, and mother has enjoyed herself vastly."

When they had reached a portion of the High Street that was clear she turned to Bladys and said:

"And now tell me all about it. You compelled them to send you out?"

"Yes, with the tolling of the alarm bell. My chamber was over the gate, and the rope was in my room. I had no other resource. I knew it would draw together a crowd, and I was also confident that it would frighten them into yielding to what I asked."

"And that was?"

"To be let go."

"You did bravely. And whither are you now going?"

"That is what I cannot say."

"Will you come with us to Kinver?"

"I have no longer a home there."

"Your father is not yet married."

"But he shortly will be; and he does not wish to have me there."

"You shall stay at the Rock Tavern till some chance arrives. George will take you back with mother and me. There is room for all. He will not refuse me that."

"I cannot go yet awhile. I have a commission to perform."

"For whom?"

"For the woman that was burnt. She laid an injunction on me."

"Will that hold you for long?"

"I cannot say. I have to go somewhere, and how far distant that place is I know not."

"Whither must you go?"

"To Nesscliffe."

"I have heard tell of the place. That is where Wild Kynaston had his cave. He was a mighty outlaw, long ago, but when—how many years are gone by since then—that is past my saying. His horse fed in a meadow under the rocks, and Wild Humphrey whistled, then his horse ran up the stair in the rock into his cave, as nimble as a squirrel. There are many stories told about that man."

"I never heard any of them. I am obliged to go to that place."

"Then I will desire George to drive us over to-morrow. Mother is a morsel tired with the excitement of to-day and the long drive from the Rock, and will be glad of a day's rest. George is certain to delight in seeing where Wild Humphrey lay hid, and whence he rode forth to rob travellers on the King's highway. Come with me. We are lodged at the Wool Pack—mother, George, and I. We are now close to the tavern. Mother is toasting her knees at the fire, laughing and crying; she has enjoyed herself prodigiously. I cannot understand it. My heart jumped towards you when you kissed the poor creature, and I felt then that I would go through fire and water to serve you. But, mother—well, she always was a strange cast of woman. I reckon there be others feel a pleasure in these executions just as does she, or they would not have come in from all the villages round. I've a knowledge some came from Bridgenorth, and we—as you see—from farther still. You should have seen how the road was covered with sightseers, walking, riding, driving, all to witness the death of one poor weak woman. Holy Austin was right. The sight of these things makes folks hard-hearted."

Quickly Nan conducted Bladys down an open passage, and through a door into a small room, in which the atmosphere was charged with fumes of tobacco and gin. A coal fire was burning in the grate, and before it, crouched in the glow, sat the hostess of the Rock Tavern. To save her holiday gown from being singed, she had turned it over her lap, and then, because her red petticoat was also too precious to be allowed to scorch, this also had been treated in like manner.

On the table stood a tumbler of spirits and water, and on the hob was a short clay pipe.

The old woman took a sip at one, and then a whiff at the other. She wore a white cap, the frills standing out as a halo about her withered yellow face, that was inflamed with spirits and the heat of the fire.

She greeted Bladys with effusion, caught her hand, patted the back of it, and then kissed her palm.

"Ha! ha! my pretty one, my mealy-face! You have seen a sight to-day. Old as I am, I have never had the chance before. Have you used the drie, as I taught you? No? When will you give it him? Have no fear. There can be no danger to you. That woman who was executed to-day was a sorry botcher. That was a bungle—giving her husband nightshade. That came of her not applying to one of us knowing ones. You were wiser. Go, my dear, and let him have a pinch in his pudding or his posset. No one will ever discover that he came by his death by foul means. If I had known who Luke Francis was he would never have left the Rock Tavern without some of it down his throat. But there, there, there," she patted the hand of Bladys again; "you have it, and will make good use of it. They will not burn you. There is no doctor in the world will be able to say that he who dies from drie has taken poison. It causes a slow wasting away; and they think, fond fools, it is a consumption."

"Mother," said Nan, "Stewponey Bla is going to return to Stourton with us."

"Ho, ho!" laughed the old woman, and her eyes twinkled. "So you have done it already. Oh, you fox, you will not admit it, even to me. You wish to be well out of the way. But I do not hold by that. Return to him, and when he becomes sick and faint, and loses colour and flesh and appetite, call in a doctor. He can do nought, but it saves appearances and turns aside suspicion. Not that they can prove anything. That they never can. Above all, put away the last pinch of the powder, lest it should be found. Yet, even if found, they would be able to make nothing of it; drie is known only to us. It is a secret among the knowing ones. I do not hold with your running away. Go back to him! Go back, I say, at once."

"I cannot return," answered Bladys. "I have been thrust out of the house. But, indeed, Mother Norris, you are in the wrong. I have given him nothing."

"Then you are a fool. Where is my drie?"

At that moment the old woman's attention was diverted by the apparition of the monkey. The door was ajar, and the hideous little face was visible, together with one hairy hand, as it peered cautiously in.

Mrs Norris crowed, chuckled, and clapped her hands.

"Beelzebub! Ha, ha! My little familiar in a red coat. You have returned to me again, after an enjoyable day's work. Sit down here on this stool at my feet, and warm thy numbed hands. Shall I teach thee to smoke?"

Then the Savoyard entered. She turned to him and asked.

"Well, Jac'mo, have you brought me the ashes?"

The man nodded, and produced a soiled rag containing charcoal.

"That is right," said the old woman. "You scraped it off the charred stake?"

"Si! Si!"

"It is sovereign against Saint Anthony's fire," said the hag, looking towards her daughter and Bladys, then back to the Italian. "Could you procure me the twist with which she was strangled? I desired that."

The man explained in broken English that the string had been consumed.

"I am sorry for that. If I could have secured it, it is preservative against the palsy, and I may be threatened with that—old people are."

Then, reverting to the topic left on the appearance at the door of the monkey, she asked again.

"Where is the drie?"

"It is here untouched," answered Bladys.

The woman took it, then looked around her, and asked.

"Where is the Captain?"

"I have not seen him lately," answered Nan.

"He ought to be here. Where is he? Why is he not with you, Nan? What business can he have in Shrewsbury, Nan? Nan, it is my belief that he is growing cold. He would desert you, I am confident, but that he is afraid."

"Afraid of what?" asked Nan; and at once her lips quivered, and her eyes filled.

"Afraid lest you should betray him."

"That, never!" answered the girl firmly.

"Well, well! we know so much; perhaps too much. Let him beware he does not trifle with us. Give me the drie. It may serve for others, if it has not been employed where intended at the first."

CHAPTER XVII. — KYNASTON'S CAVE

Out of the great Shropshire plain, south of Ellesmere, rises a fragment of red sandstone which has for the most part been swept away by the ancient Severn Sea.

This fragment must have been composed of harder rock than the rest of the bed, and it stood up above the waves a sheer cliff on one side, sloping rapidly into the water on the other. Now it is, as its name implies, a Ness—in shape a nose—and at the end of last century was clothed with heather and short grass, except only where precipitous, and it rose above the woodland that constituted the Shropshire plain.

Some thirty or forty years ago it was planted with Scotch fir and larch, and the precipitous face is largely screened by the growth of pines and beech. Moreover, what was common land has been hedged about, and padlocked gates deny freedom of passage over the preserve.

In the reign of Henry VII. there lived a certain Humphrey Kynaston at Middle Castle, not far from Nesscliffe, and of this castle he was Constable under the Crown. He sadly neglected his duties. He allowed the fortress to fall into disrepair, almost into ruin. Finding himself short of money, he took to highway robbery. The Wars of the Roses had left an element of anarchy in the land, and every man deemed himself at liberty to exercise his hand against his fellow, if that fellow should be weaker than himself and have something covetable about him.

The story is told that one day he rode to the Manor House of the Lloyds of Aston, and asked for a draught of wine. With ready hospitality a silver bowl was produced brimming with the juice of the grape. Humphrey, who was mounted, drained the goblet to the last drop, then, striking spurs into his horse, he galloped away, carrying the silver vessel with him.

His depredations became at length so notorious that he was decreed an outlaw. Kynaston was now obliged to leave the dilapidated Castle of Middle. He sought himself a place of refuge, and found it in the face of the cliff at Ness. In this cliff, the base of which is reached by a rapid ascent, and which shoots some seventy feet above the debris, he cut a flight of steps along a projecting buttress till he reached the main face, and into this he tunnelled. First he bored a doorway, then he excavated chambers, one to serve as a stable for his horse, the other as a habitation for himself. In the latter he formed a fireplace, scooped in the living rock, with a chimney above it for the escape of smoke. Beside his doorway he cut a window. The entrance was closed by a stout door of oak, sustained by a couple of massive bars.

At the foot of the cliff, near the first step, is a trough dug out of the rock, not to receive water, but corn for the horse, brought by Kynaston's mother. This lady, on hearing of her son's outlawry, came to reside in the neighbourhood, and every Saturday she left Ruyton, where she lived, with a supply of provisions for her son and his horse, sufficient to last through the week. Sunday was a day of civil freedom.

From his place of refuge in the face of the crag Humphrey carried on his depredations. It was said of him, as of Robin Hood, that he preyed only on the rich; but this fact, if fact it be, does not greatly tend to qualify his misconduct, as one principal reason why he should not plunder the poor would be that they had nothing of which to despoil them. Another was, that it was to his interest to enlist the sympathies of those living in close proximity, who might, if ill-disposed, easily betray him.

Humphrey on one occasion had been marauding on the farther side of the Severn, when the under-sheriff of the county, at the head of a posse, obtaining wind thereof, rode out to arrest him. For this purpose he placed his men in ambush beside Montford Bridge, and removed several planks from the farther side of the structure. By this bridge Kynaston was expected to return. In due course the outlaw appeared on the bank, and unsuspiciously rode on to the bridge; whereupon the posse-comitatus rose up and occupied the bridge end he had passed, cutting off his retreat, and believed that they had him now securely entrapped. But the outlaw spurred his horse, which leaped the gap, and he escaped. The leap was measured, marked out on Knockin Heath, and cut in the turf with his initials at each end.

Two or three years after his outlawry, Humphrey Kynaston was pardoned, May 20th, 1493; and the pardon is still extant, in the possession of Mr. Kynaston of Hardwick Hall, the representative of this venerable and historic family.

The distance from Shrewsbury in a north-westerly direction is but eight or nine miles, over the bridge of Montford, the scene of Kynaston's exploit.

Shropshire is a county of distant views, and these of the noblest description. From Nesscliffe a matchless prospect is obtained of the Welsh mountains, rising up like a stormy sea tossed into waves to receive the setting sun. To the south, starting out of the well-wooded plains, shoot the two cones of Breidden, and farther away, in a blue and vaporous distance, stretches the bank of the Long Mynd.

On the morning following the escape of Bladys from the Gate House, George Stracey drove Nan Norris and her to Nesscliffe. He and Nan sat in front, in the singular market-cart conveyance in which they had made their journey to Shrewsbury. Behind were two seats, on one of which was Bladys.

George Stracey was in boisterous spirits, but Nan was depressed, and her eyes gave indications of tears having been shed plentifully during the night. At a short distance from the foot of the sandy slope below Nesscliffe was an old inn; and here Stracey put up the horse, and ordered a meal to be prepared against his return from Kynaston's Cave.

Then all three started to climb the ascent, over heather and whin, and reached the crag without impediment.

Bladys was not a little embarrassed by the presence of her companions. Her errand was one that she could execute only when alone. Nan and Stracey had exhibited some curiosity about it, and had plied her with questions, to which she had given evasive answers; and she feared lest they should keep too near her the whole time she was at Nesscliffe, or so watch her as to prevent her discharge of the commission with the secrecy she desired, and which had been imposed upon her.

The stair in the rock consisted of twenty-six steps, conducting to the doorway that opened some sixteen feet above the base of the crag; and this was wide enough to allow of one only mounting at a time, nor could this be effected without some danger, as it was unprovided with a hand-rail, and some of the steps were worn in the soft sandstone, and were slimy with oozing water and algoid growths.

George Stracey led the way, and on reaching the door, extended a hand to assist Nan to enter.

Immediately opposite was a pier, dividing the cavern into two chambers; that on the left served formerly as the stable, and that on the right, of ampler dimensions, was the habitation of the outlaw himself.

In the dividing pier were cut two niches, presumably to contain lamps, and between them his initials and the date 1564; not indeed in Kynaston's own cutting, but inserted thirty years after his death, which had occurred in 1534, and more than seventy years after his occupancy of it.

Bladys entered last, and looked observantly about her. She at once noticed the fireplace cut in the rock; and the light falling from above on the hearth revealed a stone slab, on which fires had been lighted in recent times, for it was heaped up with wood ashes, and the charred ends of heather and whin lay around it.

After Nan and George Stracey had sufficiently examined the cave, amidst laughter and allusions thrown out, which were comprehensible between themselves, but which Bladys neither could nor cared to understand, all re-descended the steps and returned to the tavern, where, in the meantime, a table had been spread, ale had been drawn in a tankard, and bacon and eggs had been fried.

As all three had good appetites, furnished by the long drive in the fresh air, the meal was found acceptable, and would have passed off without hitch but for one disturbing element.

This was the girl who served—a tall, comely lass, whose hair was cut short and curled about the temples. This unusual feature gave piquancy to her appearance, which her other attractions hardly deserved. She possessed, however, a pair of dark eyes, which she used with effect, though not on the two girls.

That George Stracey looked in her direction, and was as fully engaged in observing her as in discussing his food, was not likely to escape the observation of Nan, whose jealousy was aroused. Gradually she lost zest in the meal, became silent, moody, and restless.

When, presently, Stracey addressed a compliment to the girl, "Od's life! I can understand Wild Humphrey quartering himself here, if in his days the wenches were half as good-looking as yourself," then Nan was unable to control herself further, and Bladys fled from the room to escape a pretty lover's quarrel.

The outbreak happened conveniently for Bladys, however painful to her, feeling as she did for Nan, as it allowed her to execute her purpose in coming to Nesscliffe, and that unnoticed by her companions.

She hastily retraced her steps to the cave, and on reaching the summit of the stair, looked about her to assure herself that she was neither observed nor pursued. Then she entered the cave, and shut the door behind her. She now plucked from her bosom the folded paper she had taken from the woman at her execution, opened it, and drew out a small key. Then she read what was written on the sheet of paper. The words were few, and not particularly explicit:

"Nesscliffe. In Kynaston's Cave. Underneath the hearthstone."

What was concealed there? Of that the paper gave no hint. Whatever it might be, Bladys assured herself that it was the wish of the dying woman that it should become her own. The last utterances of the poor creature had been sufficiently plain. Each word had burned itself into her memory. "It is for you. I cannot die with the secret. You have been good to me. You alone have pitied me. I have no one else to whom to give it. It is all for you!"

As Bladys studied the scrawl, she recalled the very intonation of the woman's voice. She saw again her face, distorted with the agony of the fear of death. She shuddered. The presence of that loving, guilty, suffering, cruelly-tortured woman was there, haunting the cave. The waft of her passion, the breath of her fear surrounded Bladys. She smelt the savour of the fire. She saw the flicker of the dancing flame. She heard the swelling roar of the voice of the multitude. She felt on her lips the clammy cheek of the victim she had kissed. Her brain reeled.

Recovering herself with an effort, she knelt at the hearth, and with some scraps of half-consumed heather swept the ashes from it, and disclosed the entire surface of the slab set in dust and ashes. It was heavy, and she was unable to lift it.

She looked about her. Behind the door was one of the bars wherewith it could be shut and fastened. She rose from her knees, fetched it, again looked forth to see that her movements were unobserved, returned to the hearth, thrust one end of the bar under the slab, and levered it from its place.

Then she saw that it covered a hollow depression, cut in the sandstone, into which a small box had been fitted, and was surrounded and half-covered with sand and cinder. The box was of wood bound with metal. It was light. She took it from its hiding-place, inserted the key in the lock—that key which had been contained in the letter—the lid yielded immediately, and by the light falling through the chimney, Bladys saw it contained jewels—twinkling, iridescent—to her inexperienced eyes, of unquestionable value. There were brooches, necklets, rings of diamonds, of pearls, and of every kind of precious stone.

Bladys at once recalled what had been told her—that the woman whose these had been was the daughter of a jeweller. This was her collection of precious ornaments, perhaps concealed in this place preparatory to flight with her lover.

Bladys hastily re-fastened the case, breathless, frightened, fearful of being seen. She replaced the hearthstone, and concealed the jewel box about her person. Then, with beating heart and bounding bosom, she returned to the door. Before descending, she looked attentively along the way to the tavern. No one was there. Probably her departure had been unobserved; or, if observed, had been welcomed as a relief by those in angry altercation.

She hastened back to the inn, and found George Stracey outside, helping to harness the horse into the conveyance. He was in a surly mood. Nan was within. Her cheeks were flushed, and her eyes sparkled with tears.

The storm had blown over, the quarrel was at an end, but it had left both ruffled and too full of their own concerns to give heed to Bladys, to ask where she had been, and wherefore she had left them.

The quarrel had left Stracey too out of humour, and Nan too unhappy for either to speak, and they mounted the conveyance in silence.

After having proceeded a mile, however, George raised the hand that held the whip, and pointed with the butt end over Nan at a house of red sandstone that had been quarried out of Nesscliffe, standing in a pleasant domain, well-timbered, and said:

"There, that's the mansion where she lived who poisoned her husband."

Neither of the girls made any observation. He continued:

"She was a jeweller's daughter, an orphan under the charge of an uncle, and he was a pig-headed old guardian. He would not suffer her to marry the young man to whom she was attached—it had been a liking begun in childhood, and he was in the army in the Netherlands. He was taken prisoner at Turcoing, and he did not get exchanged for some years. Her uncle suppressed his letters, and persuaded his niece that her lover had fallen. Then, whilst she was in despair, he so wrought upon her as to induce her to marry the owner of that house I have pointed out to you. He was a man of some family, and she of none; he was old enough to be her father. She had inherited some money—how much, I know not. After she was married the lover returned to England, and then only did she discover that she had been deceived. He was a soldier, and reckless, and persuaded her to run away with him; and she poisoned the old man. I do not think that the lover had any part in that; indeed, some say that she did not purpose doing more than giving the old fellow a draught to make him ill and keep his chamber, or to sleep, but she made the dose too strong. He slept never to wake again. That is a pretty seat for a gentleman, and not such as a fellow would care to leave, especially if he had a young, fresh, and pretty wife.

"Whether she was handsome or not, I cannot tell; we could not get near enough to the stake to see. And with the fear of death—and such a death—it was not likely that then she would look her best, eh, Nan? There, do you mark yonder park palings? That is the limit of the domain. They assured me at the tavern yonder that she had been a sweet and well-disposed lady, and that none hereabouts gave credence that she had purposed to kill her husband. Who will come into the estate now is doubtful. The old man had no near relatives, and as to what was hers there also is a doubt. The property of one who dies for petty treason is confiscated to the State; but hers, doubtless, had been joined to and disposed of by her husband, so the Crown could not lay hands on it. It is well there were no children, for this sentence carries with it corruption of blood. They tell me she had jewels which were given her by her father, or left to her, but what became of them, and who would claim them, none knew. If I knew where they were, and could reach them—eh, Nan?"

"See now," exclaimed Nan, whose good humour had returned, "we have quitted Nesscliffe, and have not been that Stewponey Bla was able to do that for which we brought her hither. What was it, Bladys? Shall we turn back?"

"On no account. I have accomplished my errand."

"It was an errand. To whom?"

"It was a commission."

"But when? How? I did not see you—"

"Do not concern yourself about me," said Bladys hastily. She was embarrassed how to answer.

Then, as George Stracey drew up, and again raised his hand, she said hastily:

"I ought to have spoken before—but yet I could not. Indeed, I did not know—not till this minute—not till the Captain pointed to the house did I observe it—my brain has been too heated and disturbed to see things. Never before have I noticed that Captain Stracey has a crooked forefinger."

"He has had that for some years," said Nan. "He received a cut across the joint, and it healed badly. What of that?"

"A vast deal," answered Bladys. "When Luke Hangman and I were stopped by the highwaymen on the heath beyond Stourton, then, if you remember, Nan, the leader of them made us foot it on the turf, and he danced as well."

"Right, so I recollect," answered the girl, and she touched her male companion, who had drawn the reins and brought the horse to a standstill.

"What then?" inquired Stracey.

"There was moonlight mingled with daylight, for the sun had not long set," continued Bladys, "and Luke Onion was able to observe attentively not only what went forward, but those who partook in the affair."

Stracey listened attentively, and an expression of uneasiness and apprehension crept over his face.

"He noticed that the head man or Captain who danced had a crooked forefinger on the right hand."

Both Nan and the driver started.

"And as Onion had been staying at the Stewponey ten days or a fortnight he had played at bowls and also at cards with sundry gentlemen of the neighbourhood, and he had made himself familiar with the name and appearance of one of these, and that was a man with a stiff and bowed forefinger."

"Go on," said Stracey. He turned in his seat and looked at the girl in the back portion of the conveyance. His face was bleached, and the hand that held the reins shook.

"He is so well assured that the highwayman who robbed him is none other than this same gentleman—I need not be shy of naming him—Mr George Stracey, that he has laid information against him and has proceeded to obtain warrants in the three—nay, four—counties, so as to make certain of being able to secure him."

Stracey uttered a terrible oath.

"Why did you not tell me this before? Why have you let me come to this cursed place, and so lose a day?"

"I was quite uncertain that the matter touched you. He mentioned no names except Baxter and Poulter. I may have entertained a half-fancy, but nothing more. I had not noticed the crooked finger of the highwayman that night; I was too greatly alarmed to notice anything. It was but last night that Luke Onion declared what he had seen and what he knew, and, further, what he proposed doing. And it was not till a minute ago, when you lifted your hand, that I perceived what ailed your forefinger on the hand that held the whip."

Stracey brought the lash across the back of the horse.

"May I die, Nan," said he, "but there is not a moment to be lost. I wish we may be back in time. Curse it, I was mad to come on this fool's errand to-day."

"Nay, George, but for this you would not have known what Luke Onion had determined against you. You may thank her that she has shown you the net before it has been drawn."

Then turning to Bladys, and allowing her to see how pale her face had become, she said:

"I pray you tell us everything you can about this matter."

"There is nothing further to relate. Luke Hangman said he was confident that the Captain with the bent forefinger who had stayed him was none other than the redoubted Poulter, otherwise called Baxter, who had been looked for so long and ineffectually; and that he now believed this man would not escape his clutches. He did not mention the name by which he was known in this neighbourhood, only that he could swear to him because of the crooked forefinger."

For the rest of the journey the horse was driven as he had probably never been pressed before. At intervals whispers passed between Stracey and Nan Norris, which Bladys did not catch, nor, indeed, did she attempt to overhear.

The face of each was grave, and every trace of recent disagreement had vanished.

Moreover, curiosity relative to the object of the journey of Bladys to Nesscliffe had been effaced from their minds in their great concern over the danger that directly menaced one of them, and indirectly the other.

The cart was driven through the streets of Shrewsbury at a furious pace, and the beast, panting and blotched with foam, was drawn up at the door of the Wool Pack.

Stracey swung himself out of the vehicle, and without regarding the women or helping them to dismount, ran into the inn, and burst into the room where sat the hostess of the Rock Tavern.

"Mother Norris!" said he, in a voice that quivered with emotion, "there's damnable news come."

"Ay! ay! I know it."

"You do?"

"You are blown."

"Why did you not tell me this earlier? before I started for Nesscliffe? I might have been halfway to Kinver by this time."

"That is fine talking. How could I tell you when he was not arrested till three hours after you were gone?"

"Arrested? Who? What is your meaning?"

"What is my meaning?" repeated the hag; "why, this—that the constables have taken him, and Beelzebub as well."

"Have arrested Jac'mo!" almost shrieked Stracey.

"Who else? They have taken him to the Castle, and the monkey with him."

"Oh, curse the monkey!" throwing himself into a chair, with an expression of dejection, almost of despair on his face. "We are lost."

"He is certain to peach," said the beldame; "I made signs to him not to understand a word of English addressed to him. He was in deadly terror. They will do with him what they like."

"He will tell everything. Curse the day that we trusted him."

"He has been useful. As Z stands at the end of the alphabet, so doth the gallows finish the life of such as you. Meet it bravely, Captain."

Stracey broke into imprecations.

"Not a moment is to be lost," said he; "Nan and I must return immediately to Kinver, with a chaise and post-horses. We must get there first."

"What will you do?"

"Clear out Meg-a-Fox Hole."

"And then?"

"Clear off myself."

"What am I to do?"

"Stewponey Bla shall drive you leisurely home to-morrow."

"As you will. It is late, and a drive in the cold night air would bring on my cough. See, a coffin has just shot out from the fire—to your feet, not to mine. It passed me—it lies smoking before you."

Stracey flung from the room to order the lightest available carriage, with the best post-horses that could be procured, to be ready immediately. To Nan he said in a low voice:

"You urge them on; I shall walk forward. You shall catch me up clear of Shrewsbury."

He walked leisurely through the town, swinging a rattan, and crossed the bridge; then passed the Abbey, without meeting with any inconvenience. In fact, the Italian had as yet told nothing, and the magistrates were profoundly ignorant that the redoubted Captain had been staying in the town.

Nan urged on the ostlers, made promises of extra payment, and said:

"The poor gentleman has just learned that his mother is dying. She has been suffering long from a consumption, and now has broke a blood vessel. He has walked ahead, so impatient is he to reach his home. He lives at Much Wenlock."

Every word was untrue, but it served the girl's purpose, and with rapidity the chaise was got ready, and the postboys arrived duly caparisoned in their jackets, breeches, and boots. Nan sprang in, and the horses started at a trot.

Not until a quarter of an hour after the departure of Nan did the old woman start from the lethargy into which she had fallen by the fire; then lifting her hands, she uttered a cry of dismay.

"What ails you, mother?" asked Bladys.

"My dear," answered the old woman in great agitation, "have you money with you?"

"Not one penny."

"Nor have I."

"Does this greatly matter?"

"It matters everything. In his haste Captain George has gone off and forgotten to pay the inn account. They will come down on me. Pay we must, or they will seize on our horse and cart, and we shall be detained here. We have been three days here, and have eaten and drunk of the best. There will be a charge of many pounds against us, and I have nothing."

Bladys mused for a moment. She understood how serious the dilemma was. Moreover, she was impatient to leave Shrewsbury.

Presently she stood up.

"Do not be uneasy, Mother Norris; I can find a way out of the difficulty, and that speedily."

Luke Onon was sitting by the fire, his feet extended, and the soles scarlet with the reflected glow as though he had been treading in blood. No less red was his face. The expression was sinister.

A flame, the reflection of that which played above the coals, danced in his eyes. His head was bound up, and the fever of his wound had produced a twitching in his hands and feet that showed, in spite of the position of repose he had assumed, that he was in a condition of inner unrest.

Now and again, he bit his fingers, gnawing the nails; and then he spread out his hands before the fire to screen his face.

To him entered his mother.

"Luke! News!"

"Well!" He did not turn his head. "Has the cat kittened?"

"Luke, we have been robbed."

"We always are being pillaged. Nicodemus is an arrant rogue."

"We have been robbed by that wench from Stewponey."

"How so? What of her?"

"Of her, nothing but what is evil. There has been a curse on us and a blight on our affairs ever since you brought her here."

"What has she taken? My grandmother's salve box, with the Queen Anne shilling on it?"

"Luke, rouse up. She has carried away all the jewellery of that woman we burnt."

"There was none for her to take. Nicodemus secured the wedding ring and guard."

"I tell you, Luke, that she has got jewellery to the value of many hundreds of pounds."

"You have had an afternoon doze, and have been dreaming, mother."

"Luke, rouse up! I have seen them. She has already sold a brooch to Purvis, the goldsmith, for sixteen guineas, and it is worth five times that amount."

The hangman was now thoroughly roused. He sat up in his chair, put his hands on the elbows, and turned himself about.

His mother approached the hearth, and said:

"I was in High Street, when I caught a glimpse of her as she went up and down, looking into shop windows. I wondered what she sought, and I watched her without allowing myself to be seen. She remained awhile in front of Purvis's shop, first; put forth her hand as though to open the door and enter, then changed her intent and walked on, still observing the windows. After a while she came on the shop of Radstone, and stayed there. She halted before no other window but that of a jeweller; not before that of a milliner or a draper. But she did not go in at Radstone's, although she seemed to have a mind to do so; instead, she returned through the street to Purvis's. Then I was certain that she intended to buy something or sell something, and, either way, it astonished me. So I drew close, where I might see. After she had entered, then, she stood with her back to the window, and there was a light inside, by which the goldsmith had been repairing some trinket. I saw her take a box from out of her pocket."

"What box?"

"None belonging to us. None I had ever seen before. She had a key and unlocked it; but apart, so that she showed none of the contents. She drew from it a glittering ornament. It was a diamond brooch. The jeweller held it to the little lamp to examine it, and then he brought it to the window that he might inspect it by the daylight, and assure himself of the water of the stones; and he further tested them with a diamond-cutter, to assure himself that they did not scratch, and so were not of paste. I drew somewhat aside, but for all that I did not remove my eyes from him and the little brooch. Presently he went back to where she was stood, and I thrust myself nearer once more, and I saw how that he was questioning her."

Then I opened the door and entered. He looked well content, and she was startled, but speedily collected herself again, cold and hard as she is—like a block of marble The man Purvis said at once to me that he was glad I had arrived; he had been offered a diamond brooch, and that it was his custom never to purchase jewellery from one with whom he was unacquainted, lest he should be brought thereby into trouble. He said that he did not question that whatever she had said was true—"

"What had she said?"

"That I asked; and she repeated her words, looking at me straight in the face."

"What said she?"

"She said that the woman that was burnt had given to her this brooch as a present and as a remembrance of her. She had stood on the heap of fuel at her side until the last moment, and the criminal had with her last words committed this brooch to her. I had myself seen how that Stewponey girl had taken something out of the bosom of the creature."

"Was it the box?"

"No, it was a letter."

"I do not comprehend how she came by the box."

"That matters not to us. It is my positive conviction that the box is a jewel-case and contained more than the one brooch. Purvis asked her whether she were your wife. She answered him: 'I am she that came to

Shrewsbury as such.' Then he turned to me and asked me if this was the truth, and I assented. What else was I to do?"

"Proceed."

"Then he offered her ten guineas for the brooch, but she hesitated about receiving that sum. After that he came to sixteen, and would advance nothing beyond. She made no offer to open the case and to show whether it contained other jewellery, although Purvis inquired whether she had many pieces to dispose of, for then he might consider if he could make the sum up to eighteen. She answered curtly that she had nothing more to sell to him. But it is my solemn belief that she has got more in the case, and I think that the goldsmith was of the same mind. I knew not what to say or do. What should I have done, Luke?"

"Go forward with your account. It matters not what has been done; provision must be made as to what is to be done next."

"There you are right, Luke. Consider yourself in my position."

"I should not have acted thus. I should have laid my hand on the case and brooch, and have said they were mine."

"I did not know what course to take. I was as one distraught. I thought that had it come out before the goldsmith that the case contained jewels of price, and that all had come from the woman that was burnt for petty treason, then the Crown might have claimed it, and we should have got nothing."

Luke considered.

"After all, it was as well. We must manage secretly—or in some other way."

"Then he handed her sixteen guineas, and without another word she left."

"And you?"

"I went with her and endeavoured to induce her to return to the Gate House—not, God wot, that I desire to have her here again, save only for so long till we have secured the case. I assured her that you were ill. The blow on your head and the events of last night had brought upon you a brain fever, and the surgeon who visited you despaired of your life. But she paid no regard to my words. Whether she believed them or not, I cannot say. She sought to shake me off, but I clung to her skirt as a burr. I asked her how many pretty trinkets she had in the case, but she gave me never a word in reply. Then she took her way over the Welsh Bridge towards Skelton and walked fast; but I knew at what she aimed, so I fell short of breath and halted and waited about in corners, watching, hidden lest she should perceive me, and an hour later, as it grew to dusk, she stole back into the town, and then I slipped from my hiding-place and followed after. Whether she had the case with her or whether she had gone to Glendower's Oak, and maybe concealed it there, I could not say. I walked after her, unperceived, and tracked her to the Wool Pack."

"She is at the Wool Pack?"

"She is. I learned there that she had been in the inn, staying with kinsfolk or acquaintances, since she left us."

"And who might those kinsfolk be? Her father has not come here with his wife; that would be too quick."

"At the Wool Pack there was a gentleman, a kind of Captain, whom they named George, and he had with him an aged gentlewoman who smacked of the witch, and of whom the folk at the inn were somewhat afraid; and there was, further, a daughter—a forward wench, called Nan."

"What!" exclaimed Luke Onion, leaping to his feet. "They in Shrewsbury! George Stracey! The very man whom I hope to hang! I will have him seized immediately."

"It is too late; he is off."

"Off? Whither?"

"To Bridgenorth or Much Wenlock. He had news that his mother was sick of a blood vessel that was broke, and that she was dying. So he called out a chaise and post-horses, and he and the girl are off."

"Girl! What girl?"

"Not Bladys; the other."

"He has slipped through my fingers, by Lucifer! He is clever, but I will have him yet. Mother, what has frightened him has been the arrest of the Italian. No time is to be lost. We must after him to-morrow."

"But what about your wife?"

"Well considered. She shall first be secured. She is on the spot. I will have a warrant out against her for deserting me, her husband. A wife, if she leaves and will not return, can be brought home by the constables. If we can get her here, then we can make the surrender of the jewels and the case the price of her freedom. As to her threats, they do not alarm me. She has set her mind to be free, and will cheerfully give up the precious stones if that will insure her against pursuit."

"The wench is in league with thieves and robbers. She went to that Captain the moment she left us. It is possible enough that the jewels have been gotten by some robbery of his, and she is attempting to pass them for him, and that the story of obtaining them from that woman was made up for the occasion."

"That also is likely. We must get her into our hands; and then leave me to force her to surrender the jewels; in whatever way she came by them, we must endeavour to get possession of them."

"For Heaven's sake, do not patch up a peace and bring her here again."

Luke laughed contemptuously.

"I have lived so long without a wife, that I can live a bachelor a little longer. The taste of matrimony I have had has been one of bitterness of wormwood. Get me my hat; I will take steps at once to seize her."

But the necessary steps were not to be taken as easily nor as readily as Luke anticipated.

The magistrate to whom he applied was at dinner, and would not be disturbed till he had consumed his accustomed bottle of port, and then was in too hilarious and confused a condition to be able at once to bring his mind to bear on the matter presented to him; nor, when he did comprehend it, was he disposed to grant the request of Onion without sundry jokes and sallies that protracted the business till late.

When finally the hangman was furnished with the requisite powers, and hastened to the Wool Pack, it was too late.

Bladys had flown. No sooner had she obtained the money she required, than she had discharged the account at the tavern, and ordered a post-horse for the conveyance left by Stracey at the inn, and had departed from Shrewsbury, taking the old woman with her.

"It matters not," said Onion. "With one hand I will sweep together the entire crew, and her with the rest."

CHAPTER XX. — THE TALLY STICK

Bladys was at the Rock Tavern, along with Mother Norris. She had perceived at once, when fastened on by Mrs Onion, that the woman and her son would make an attempt to secure her, so as to get possession of the case of jewellery.

To escape from Shrewsbury as quickly as possible was her obvious course, and on her return to the Wool Pack, she at once engaged a post-boy and horses. To the old woman, she explained the urgency of the case; George Stracey's beast was to be left in the inn stable till called for. She discharged the account in full, and departed the same night. After her arrival at the Rock Tavern, her mind sank into inactivity. A sort of moral paralysis took possession of her, much as before the marriage. She was aware that she was brought into association with undesirable persons; that the old woman was vicious at heart, and a source of evil in her neighbourhood; and that the relation in which Nan stood to George Stracey was not respectable. She was, moreover, alive to the fact that the man was a notorious highwayman, and that the Rock Tavern was a meeting-place for bad characters. But whither could she go? She was without friends. The only house on which she had any claim was the Stewponey Inn, and to that she neither could nor would return.

It was characteristic of Bladys that she acted with resolution and without hesitation, so long as she saw a way before her. She did not always take that course which was recommended to her, but that which approved itself to her mind, and was consistent with her notions of right and wrong. But she was destitute of imagination, lacking in initiativeness. Under the circumstances, a weak character would have yielded to hysterics, and have fallen into a condition of depression stupefying to the mind.

With her this was not the case. Her will was at a standstill, and her faculties in abeyance. She was like one who is proceeding along a road, and arrives at a point where several ways diverge, and there is no sign-post. The wise traveller, instead of dashing along a road that may be wrong, tarries for the arrival of someone who can give him the desired direction. His force of mind and will are not gone from him, but brought to a condition of inaction and expectancy.

A girl with lively imagination would have had her head in a ferment with a thousand schemes of escape from the untoward predicament—schemes practicable and impracticable—jostling each other, overthrowing each other; and would have adopted that scheme which obtained the mastery over the others at the moment when a selection had to be made. But Bladys had not this tumid brain, full of the germs of ideas, and when she lost her way she stood still and waited. She had been roused from such a condition before, when in the Rock Tavern, by the advice of Mother Norris, who had given her a packet of poison wherewith to rid herself of the husband she did not love, so as to be able to surrender herself to the man whom she did.

Bladys had not for a moment entertained the thought of acting on this advice, but the words of the hag had suggested to her the possibility of working on the fears of her husband so as to induce him to relinquish his rights over her. A way out of the dilemma had been shown her; she took, not that pointed out, but a parallel course.

Now, again, she had come to an "impasse." She was associated with undesirable characters, and she saw no way of freeing herself from this association. She could not go back to her father without a sacrifice of her pride. But to remain in the Rock Tavern was also wounding to her self-respect. Nan had been more than kind to her. The girl's warm and tender heart had opened to Bladys. She was grateful for this kindness, and she was unwilling to do anything to wound poor Nan. She recognised good qualities in the girl; she saw that with other associations, and with a better bringing up, she would have been a good woman; but Bladys could not shut her eyes to what was bad, nor seem to condone her more than equivocal position.

What was she to do? Whither could she go? She could do nothing, go nowhere. So, seeing her helplessness, she sank into an impassive, waiting condition.

Nan showed herself but little at the Rock Tavern. She was much away, returning home at irregular intervals only. During Nan's absence, Bladys actively assisted in the work of the house, to relieve the old woman, and do something to repay the hospitality shown her.

Her nerves had been overstrung. The events that have been recorded followed each other with rapidity, and without a pause in which her jaded powers could be given time to recover themselves.

This, added to the consciousness of being in a false position, from which she saw no way of escape, helped to produce in Bladys a condition of semi-sleep, to deprive her of elasticity of mind and spirit.

When not at work for the house, she was not occupied with her thoughts. In another woman, the brain would have been in action. With her it stood still, like a clock of which the weights have run down. Nan, coming in, saw the condition in which she was, and divining that something was wrong, without being able to understand the difficulties of Bladys, misinterpreted her mood; and, after a whispered conference with her mother, she said—

"Wait, Bla! I know what aileth thee, and will send the doctor."

Then she whisked off.

There was nothing for Bladys to do in the house; not a person came to the tavern—it seemed to have no custom. Consequently, to be away from the objectionable cackle of the old woman, Bladys went to her bedroom.

A robin had lost its way, and was in the chamber. It fluttered from place to place, and perched, now on the cupboard, then on the top of an open door; anon it made a dash at the window, stunned itself momentarily, then rose, beat with its wings against the pane, abandoned the attempt, returned to its flitting about the room, to the cupboard, to the door, and once again to precipitate itself against the pane.

The door was open, a ready way of escape offered, yet the bird never essayed that. It directed all its efforts towards escape by the way that was impracticable, with the invariable result of being struck back by the glass.

It was much the same with Bladys; or rather it had been so. If her mind had risen, spread wings, and attempted to reach the light, it had smitten against an obstacle, and had fallen back stunned.

She watched the robin, and then opened the casement, to allow the bird to escape. As she did so she heard the strident tones of the old woman calling below for her to come down.

She obeyed, and descending the stair, saw Mother Norris in the kitchen, holding a stick towards her.

"See here, Stewponey Bla," said the beldame, "I have made your life tally with Luke Hangman. Would you have another tally? Then you must burn the first. Come to the hearth. Seat yourself on the farther side, on the stool of Beelzebub. Take the tally and consider it well. I am a witch—or know something of dealings with spirits—and I have more power than some will allow. Come now, you shall prove it Take this tally, and I swear to you that before you have burnt it, he whom you desire to see will appear. I will lead him to you. But you can begin no fresh tally with him until that with Luke Hangman is finished. See, wench, see! It is bound about with threads; and every bond must be snapped by fire, and as the last gives way, and the half-stick falls from its place, he—that other one, shall appear."

Bladys looked at Mrs Norris without understanding what she meant. To the mantelshelf on both sides of the fire were slung bundles of hazel rods, each eighteen inches in length. A hole drilled with a red hot skewer through the end of each allowed a string to be passed through, and to form a loop by which the rod was suspended. At this end of suspension, which was the handle, was a symbol, different in each. Four inches from the extremity a cut had been made diagonally from right to left, extending half-way through the stick, and the rod had then been split from the farther extremity to this cut. By this means, a half of each rod had been removed. Along the edges of the split were notches made by a knife.

Mistress Norris not only kept a tavern, but she did a small business in muffins, simnel, and short-cakes, that she baked; and as she and the majority of her customers were ignorant of the art of ciphering, their accounts were kept by means of tallies.

Each customer preserved the half-piece of his peculiar tally, and when he came for cake brought his piece of wood with him. This was applied to the portion preserved in the kitchen, and notches were cut in both, according to the muffins or cakes supplied. By means of the two portions of the stick, dealer and customer had corresponding accounts which could not be falsified.

In a drawer of the kitchen table Mother Norris kept tally sticks ready for use when the old were full, and the accounts settled, or when fresh customers arrived.

One of these she had drawn forth, and had bound it about with various scraps of thread and coloured wool.

The old woman thrust this stick into the girl's hand.

"Dost understand, wench? This is thy Staff of Life along with Luke Hangman. Of this thou must loosen every tie afore thou begin another staff with him of whom thou thinkest. You said once to me, 'I do not love Luke—I love another.'"

Bladys made no remark; only a flicker of sudden illumination came into her dreamy eyes.

"See," continued the crone. "Here I cut a notch." With the sharp knife that she had been whetting on the hearthstone she chipped a piece from the wood at the junction of the parts. "That is your father's promise to Luke. Here I cut another—that is his winning you; here a third—you take his hand; and again I nick it, there—you swear before God to be his, and his only."

"I did not swear," said Bladys gravely.

"And here I make another notch," continued the old woman. "This is where he puts the ring upon your hand."

"I have no ring. I plucked it off, and left it in Shrewsbury."

"And here I cut a gash to signify the blessing of the parson. 'What God hath joined together, let not man put asunder.' Let see, but devils can do that; ay, and I likewise. And here is the registration of your marriage in the parish books. See—between this band and that next we have all these tally marks. Now we make way beyond. Here again I nick out a piece—it signifies that he has put his arms about you and called you his own."

"That he never did."

"And here," chipping again, "is the virginal kiss from your pretty lips—the seal of marriage."

"It was never sealed."

"And here again," continued the old woman, "he receives you into his house and makes it your home."

"I have left it."

"Take the tally. I know no more. You contradict me in all. Thrust the end into the fire till it is well kindled, then hold it upright before and let it burn as a taper. Let it burn on steadily, snapping band after band, and devouring tally mark after tally mark, and I swear unto you that when the last band breaks and the half-stick falls he will come."

Bladys, hardly understanding the old creature, obeyed her directions. She seated herself on a stool by the hearth, she accepted rather than took the rod thrust upon her, and following the instructions of the crone thrust the extremity among the red-hot ashes. Instantly the hazel stick burst into yellow flame. Bladys then withdrew it, and remained seated, holding the staff as if it had been a torch before her. A blue flame leaped and wavered at the end of the tally, then broke into a spurt of golden light. Snap! one of the bands gave way, and the glowing ring fell on the floor. The flame at the end of the rod gathered force, it ate its way down, nibbling at each notch with blue lips, then gulping at the portion of stick in which it was cut and proceeding to attack the next.

"He is coming this way," said the hag. "Hist! hist!" She made a sign as if beckoning with her finger.

"It burns bravely," laughed the old woman. "By Goles! this is not such a wedding tally as needs much fire to loose it. There goes another band."

Bladys now became interested or amused, much as might a child, in what took place. She gave no heed to the words of Mrs Norris.

"Hush! I hear his step," laughed the hag. "As the husband retires the lover approaches."

"I have no husband," said Bladys.

"You have not done with him yet; not till the last bond is broken and the stick falls."

"I have never had one."

"That is purely!" The old woman fell a-cackling, and still she beckoned. "I am drawing him nearer. This tally will soon be broken; then you shall begin a new account."

The fire reached the last tie; it had swallowed the last notch. Pieces of charcoal fell off the consumed portion. Suddenly the final band flamed, and the two portions of the stick fell apart, and Bladys cast her handled piece on the hearth. At that moment the window was partially obscured by a passing figure.

Bladys started to her feet. The door opened, and a man stood on the threshold.

With a cry she reeled; she had recognised him, and would have fallen unconscious on the floor had she not been caught in the arms of Crispin Ravenhill.

CHAPTER XXI. — A PROTECTOR

Whether Bladys passed into unconsciousness wholly, or only trembled on the edge, that she knew not; nor how long she had been in the arms of Crispin—whether a moment, whether an eternity.

In the joy, delirium, insensibility succeeding each other, all sense of time was lost to Bladys. It was not that love had transported her into a new world, but it was love combined, interwoven with the certainty that she had reached the limit of her trials; that in him she had a guide out of the labyrinth and darkness into which she was cast, and from which unaided extrication was impossible. She was as one drowning, who frantically clings to the one object that can alone save him from being engulfed.

Whether she were awake or asleep, alive or dead, that she knew not, in the supreme ecstasy of consciousness that she was safe. She felt strong arms about her, a beating heart smiting against hers, and hot lips pressed against her cheek.

Returning to her senses, she was aware of the hag leaping and dancing, with a nimbleness for which she would not have credited her, waving the tally stick, that now smoked, then flamed, and screaming out a song, the words of which were unintelligible to her. Bladys turned her head on Crispin's arm, and looked at her; then the woman curtsied and said:

"The old staff is done for, and the old account is closed. We must begin the other."

Then throwing the end of the stick into the fire, she said:

"You think only of each other. I have to mind the cow," and she stumbled out of the tavern door.

By this time Bladys was sufficiently restored to disengage herself from the arms of Ravenhill, to stand back, to cover her face with her hands, and gasp for breath.

He took a step forward; she retreated.

"Bladys!" said he, "I know all. Nan Norris has told me everything."

"Not everything," she answered; "because she did not know all."

"She told me sufficient to let me understand that you have been cruelly deceived, and grossly ill-treated."

"Crispin," said Bladys, lowering her hands from her face, "that man Luke married a lump of ice only, without eyes wherewith to see, or ears to hear. I never swore to be his. What took place passed before me as a scene in a play, weighed on me as a nightmare. I solemnly assure you that I made to him no promise of love, honour, or obedience. I never said that I would take him for better or for worse. The service was gabbled over me as over a corpse, and I had as little active part therein as a corpse in the office for the dead. He did not give his true name; he concealed his profession. The utmost measure of my consent was to be taken to Shrewsbury with intent to be a servant in his house. I had made my resolve when at the Rock Tavern. When I went to Shrewsbury my mind was made up, and I placed the alternative to them, to take me as a serving-maid or to let me go."

"I understood as much from Nan."

"Before I left the Rock I said to Nan and her mother that no power on earth or under the earth would ever make me his wife; and that before I had learned what his profession was."

"Yes," said Crispin, with a smile, "that was not all you said to Nan."

"Not all!" echoed Bladys. Then a sudden flush came over her throat, cheeks, and temples, like an aurora.

"No," said Crispin, "that was not all. There was something more. You told Nan that he, Luke Hangman, had not won you; he had taken a base advantage over the man who should have been the victor, and would but for that have won the prize."

Bladys covered her face again. Then, with an effort, she raised her head, lowered her hands, and said:

"Crispin, it was my fault. It was I who spun the jack across the lawn so as to trip you up. It was through me that you fell, through me that you were stunned."

"And but for that I would have claimed you."

"Crispin, I did it not purposely. I was in a dream; I was beside myself; I was in the moon."

"It remains with you to undo what you did wrong on that day and give your heart to him who really won you."

"Crispin," she panted with labouring breath, "it has been yours throughout. If you will—"

He interrupted the words. He did not ask what she was about to say.

"If I will!" he shouted. "I have had but one thought, and that of you; but one despair, that I had lost you; entertained but one hate, and that against him who snatched you from me. I have now but one triumph, that now you are mine."

His breast heaved, his eyes darted lightnings.

"Bladys!" said he, "men will believe that you were his wife; if you come with me they will condemn you."

"Let them condemn. You know that I was not his wife."

"Bladys, we must away from this place. Here we could not be married. We must go where we are unknown. I can not say where it may be, but far from here."

"Crispin, I will go with you anywhere. I never did marry that man. It was all a hideous mockery, in which I took no willing, no consenting part."

Then he caught her in his arms and covered her face with kisses, till hands were laid upon him, and a voice sounded in his ears and bade him desist. He looked up in confusion, angry, and saw Holy Austin before him.

The old schoolmaster-knobbler gently but firmly separated his nephew from Bladys, and said:

"Crispin, your grandmother was a remarkable woman. She could not read, she knew little of the Scriptures, yet was a pious and God-fearing woman. But she had some strange notions about matters, such as have no warranty in Holy Writ, and this was one of her notions. She said to me when I was a little lad at her knee, i' feck, I had hard work afterwards to set what she told me aside for the truth as revealed. This is what she related to me of the beginning of mankind. She said that the Almighty had created the world, and had made the flowers of surpassing beauty, had painted the wings of the butterfly, and had given to the birds their melody. And He resolved to sum up in one creation all the perfections distributed among the other creatures; one to be the sovereignest of all. Then lo! He made Woman. And she was all that could be imagined of beauty and delicacy and grace. But He saw that she was frail. Then He said He would make a stick for her support,—and He proceeded to create Man."

The old man, with shrewdness, had given his nephew time to recover his composure, time also for the vapour of passion to rise from off his brain.

"So will I understand grandmother's story, uncle," said Ravenhill. "Here is my flower, and I will be her stay."

"My good Crispin," said the old man, "consider well how you set about it. In place of being the support to your flower, you will be the stick that will beat her down, break and cast her on the soil."

"How say you?"

"Bound to you she cannot be, so long as she is attached to Luke Onion."

"That was no marriage at all."

"That I know, perhaps better than you. Irregular and profane the proceeding was. Of that there can be no doubt! Nevertheless, in the eyes of everyone in Kinver and the neighbourhood she was married to that man. Until such a marriage be dissolved or proclaimed null, by lawful authority, she cannot be bound to you without such a sacrifice as you would have no right to ask of her. I ask you, nephew, if you took her to you, would you not defraud her of that which Luke Hangman could not deprive her of."

"What mean you?"

"Her good name."

Ravenhill stood motionless, absorbed in thought

"Look you, Crispin," proceeded the schoolmaster; "let it be granted that in our eyes the wedding in Stourton Chapel was nought—was in fact illegal—nevertheless you cannot take her to you as wife without an ill name attaching to her, and all respectable women will hold aloof from her. She will have no companions but the abandoned and godless. You love her?"

"Indeed, indeed I do!" answered the young man with fervour.

"Then respect her. A love that is without respect is most volatile. As certain dyes are fixed by salt, so is love made fast for life by reverence." Crispin looked up and would have spoken, but was checked by something that rose in his throat. "You are the stick to this fair lily. Very well. First let it be made clear to the whole world that the Stourton marriage was nought—and that can be established without a doubt—then in God's name marry her."

"You are right, uncle," said the young man; "I give you my hand. I promise to abide by your advice."

"That is well: the matter is not difficult. Already the churchwardens have presented a complaint against the vicar for his conduct in this very matter. The matter will be inquired into in the bishop's court, and what the result will be cannot be doubted."

"I thank you, uncle; but consider. Bladys has no adviser, no helper. She is here in a house that is not of good repute, among persons who are not seemly and suitable companions."

"Let not that concern you. I will be the temporary support. That is to say, Crispin, I will take charge of her, protect her, advise her; she shall come to no harm under my—I will not say roof, for I have none—under my rock. She shall live in the adjoining habitation to mine."

"I thank you with my whole heart," said Bladys, and held out her hand to the old man. "And now one proof of my putting entire confidence in you."

She produced the case of jewellery, and placed it in the hands of the schoolmaster. He opened it and viewed the contents with surprise.

"How came you by these?" he asked.

She informed him. Then she added:

"I desire to have them sold. To me they are valueless, but turned into money they may help—"

She looked at Ravenhill.

"Will you be wholly guided by me?" asked the Knobbler.

"Entirely."

"Then," said he; "we will first have the jewels, as they are, handed over to whomsoever it may be that represents the Crown. A person sentenced for higher petty treason forfeits everything to the Crown. It may be, however, that the right to them may not be established, as a woman's property goes to her husband, and his is not forfeited; or it may be that the Crown will waive its right. Let all be done above board."

"As you think fit."

"Then this is what I decide. Let Crispin depart at once for London with these jewels. What their worth is I do not pretend to guess. Let him there state the whole case for you, and abide by the result, whatever it may be."

Holy Austin considered a moment, and then handed the box to his nephew, said:

"Crispin, be off immediately. Now that Bladys is coming to me, it behoves you to be absent. As the Apostle advises, 'Avoid even the appearance of evil!'"

"I go, uncle. Farewell, Bla!"

In another minute he was gone.

Then entered Mother Norris, carrying a faggot for the fire. She looked first at Bladys, then at Austin, and, dropping the wood, burst into strident laughter.

"I left a young man here, and find an old one, and that Holy Austin!"

"I am come to take Stewponey Bla away with me to my rock," said the schoolmaster.

"I thank you with all my heart for the goodness you have shown me," said the girl. "But, indeed, Mother Norris, I must go. Tell Nan that I will not omit to thank her when I have the chance to see her."

Then Bladys pressed money on the old woman, who clutched it eagerly; and, after a few more words, she and the old schoolmaster departed.

"Did that woman know about the jewels?" asked the old man, when on the road at a distance from the tavern.

"She has not a suspicion."

"Well for you. Had Mother Norris known that you had such trinkets of value she would have murdered you in your bed to get possession of them."

CHAPTER XXII. — HOLY AUSTIN ROCK

At the opening of this story something was said of the curious isolated and inhabited rock, like a huge tooth, that bears the name of Holy Austin.

This detached mass, rising some seventy feet high, stands on the slope below the headland of Kinver Edge, of which at some remote period it formed a buttress. It is honeycombed with dwellings, of which there are ten, in three storeys; the topmost have their faces built up in gables, but the chambers are all excavated in the rock. Originally there was no such face of masonry, but the disintegration of the screen of sandstone by weather and rough usage made it necessary to so front it. The lowest storey or ground floor opens on the same face, the east, and is almost on a level with the hillside, at all events at one point; but the middle storey is reached by a track in the face of the cliff, that falls away on the west in a manner so precipitous that these cave dwellings are accessible only by the ledge. Of the ten habitations, some of which have more than two rooms, only four are occupied at the present time; three are void, and the rest have crumbled into ruin.

As the old schoolmaster ascended the slope to reach his own dwelling, which occupied the summit of the crag, he said to Bladys:

"Did you perceive that there was a stir in Kinver? Many persons were in the street."

"I thought as much," answered the girl.

"There is great commotion in the place, for all the constables in the neighbourhood, not in Staffordshire alone, but in the adjoining portions of Shropshire and Worcestershire, have been called out. Moreover, additional trustworthy men have been sworn in for the occasion by the magistrates, who are stirring, and have, if I may so express it, taken the field at length against the highwaymen who have infested the country, and made travelling on the Irish road so dangerous. Justitia pallida irâ, as I may say, hath at length drawn her sword."

Bladys started. She felt a flutter of alarm for Stracey, or rather, for Nan Norris. The man himself was odious to her; insolent, with vulgar affectation, and devoid of good qualities. But what touched him touched also Nan; and to the latter Bladys was grateful and attached.

"If it had not been for this," said the old man, "you would not have been suffered to traverse Kinver unquestioned. You would have been catechised along the entire street. Now the good folk of Kinver are exercised in mind about the raid; some favourably inclined towards these scourges of the country, finding it to their interest in sundry ways, and therefore scheming how they may throw impediments in the way of the ministers of Justice. When I heard that the attempt was about to be made, and also learned that you were at the Rock Tavern, I thereupon resolved in my mind to go thither, and to move you thence before it was visited. For you to have been found in that harbour of thieves and footpads might, and probably would, have done injury to your reputation."

"I thank you with all my heart."

"And now," continued the old fellow, "here shall be your home for awhile. I cannot say with the Psalmist, 'your rest for ever'—for I trust ere long another man will claim you and carry you elsewhere. We make our nest in the rock as turtles, or as Samson in Etam. There is no prospect of the constables visiting here, nor need we fear them should they scrutinise us and our tenements. As Vacuus cantat coram latrone viator, so does the honest man whistle unfluttered by the approach of the officers of the law. All who occupy this crag partake somewhat of the harmlessness and guilelessness of doves. We live by labour of the hand or head."

He had mounted with the girl to the topmost platform, and here rose the walled front of his habitation; adjoining it were other dwellings, but they were unoccupied.

He opened the door of his house, and said:

"This is the place which I inhabit, solus de superbis, but I cannot accommodate you, nor would you find it reposeful in this place; for it is my school, where I instruct children in the rudiments of religion, of English, and some of the ablest boys I even advance into Latin—rudimentary, of course. They are not old enough, or capable enough, of more than a smattering, or, to be more exact, of having the foundations laid on which they may build later when opportunity arrives. The children are here all day. Adjoining is a second house. Therein you will find quiet."

He opened the door of the cave adjoining his own, and led Bladys inside.

"You will see," said he, "that there is an advantage afforded here that exists in none other dwelling in this rock."

He pushed forward, from one chamber excavated in the sandstone to another deeper in the rock than the first, and to the girl's surprise she saw that it had window and door in the face of the cliff opposed to the entrance by which she had been admitted.

"You have a habitation that is a complete perforation of the rock. From the one side you can enjoy the sight of the rising, from the other that of the setting, sun. Only this caution must I enforce. See you do not step forth unawares—for an unconsidered and inconsiderable stride would take you out of this world into the next."

He opened the door in the western face, and led Bladys forth. He showed her a narrow ledge that ran to the left only, along the face of the precipice. The cliff rose sheer above, and fell away below, not perpendicularly, but so as to overhang. By this means, any rubbish cast out from the back door over the edge fell clear of the range of dwellings below, as also of the path that led to them. No railing, no protection of any sort, was provided along the verge.

"You can creep by the pathway to the left, if it please you, for some distance," said the Knobbler; "it anciently led to where a former occupant of this cottage kept pigeons. But the fall of a piece of the cliff has destroyed the pigeonry—or has so in part. Since I have had these two houses I have had no time to give to the keeping of birds—such pigeon-holes as remain have been invaded by jackdaws, and the track is broken and has become dangerous. I will inform you why this tenement is no longer occupied. The former dweller therein—that is, twenty years ago—had a little daughter of thirteen, whom he loved as the apple of his eye. She was much distressed that the rock had fallen, and had carried away the place where her pigeons had dwelt, and this brooded on her mind. One night she took to sleep-walking, and came in her night-shift along this very path. Something—a premonition, or the draught of the open door—aroused her father, and he came forth to see his child ascending where the ledge was broken, all white in the moonlight. He could not go to her; he dared not recall her; nay, not make a sound, lest it should waken her. One false step, one loose stone that yielded, and his child would be precipitated below, and he would take in his arms thereafter only a corpse. So he stood, trembling, sick at heart, but lifting his soul to God, that He would give His angels charge over her, lest she should dash her foot against a stone. And He did preserve her. She reached the summit, and there—there awoke, strained to the heart of her father, whose hair next morning was found to have been blanched by his great anxiety."

The old man pointed to the ascent made by the sleeping child, and Bladys shuddered. Holy Austin went on:

"As I have my school in the other house, where also I sleep, I do what little cooking I require in the habitation I now surrender to you. And now I must depart, and leave you to make yourself acquainted with your domain. I am concerned to see the result of this campaign against the highwaymen and footpads."

Then, before he departed, he said:

"You will find here a bed. It is one that I have retained for Crispin when he has been able to visit me. But, indeed, he has not much leisure, being engaged on the canals. Nevertheless, now and again, on a Sunday, he visits me, and is ever welcome. He is a good lad, and has picked up some learning from me."

Then the old man departed.

Bladys was now all alone in her rock dwelling. She seated herself on a stool to compose her thoughts. From the great anxiety that had oppressed her she was at length relieved, and her thoughts began to flow as if released by a thaw.

The good old man, whom, in spite of his pedantry, she liked and reverenced, had come to her as an angel, delivering her from an embarrassing situation. He had done more: he had saved her from herself. She was now able to repose after the strain of mind and nerve to which she had been subjected, and she could rest in hope of a happy issue from her troubles, for Holy Austin was not the man to encourage favourable expectations without good grounds. She leaned her head on her hand, enjoying the repose.

Then, recovering herself, she looked around the chamber in which she was. It was the innermost apartment, and was wholly scooped out of the rock. The western face was but a screen of natural stone, perforated artificially for window and door.

The rock was dry, as dry as are the walls built of quarried stone. Indeed, the occupants of such habitations made no complaint of damp. The only occasion on which moisture formed on their walls was when a sudden change ensued from cold weather to a warm and damp wind from the south-west. The ceiling was slightly arched, and that, as well as the sides, was whitewashed. The floor was of the bare red rock, somewhat uneven, as traffic between the doors had worn down the stone.

In the first room was a fireplace with chimney bored in the stone, much resembling that in Kynaston's Cave. In the inner compartment or room the window was small and glazed with bull's-eyes. It admitted little light, so that the chamber was gloomy as a vault.

Bladys threw open the door, as the sun was in decline, to allow its light to flood and warm the cave. She stepped out on the ledge.

A gentle breeze played with the light short hair on her brow, and fanned her cheek, like a light hand caressing her and promising peace to her troubled soul. The wind sang in a Scotch fir rooted in the red cliff overhead. She looked up, and saw the dark green mass, sustained on its red-gold stem, sway against the deep blue sky. The evening sun was on the rock, and had turned it into a mass of solidified flame.

Jackdaws flew out of the rock and wheeled or darted about her, uttering resentful cries addressed to her as a stranger. They were knowing birds, and were familiar with the inhabitants of the rock, and entertained a mistrust of the children who came there to be schooled; they lived in unintermittent strife with the boys, whom they screamed at and scolded whenever they approached. Now, in Bladys, they perceived an entire stranger, and they expressed their disapproval of her intrusion loudly and objurgatively. Was she expected by the saucy birds to pay her footing with a piece of carrion or some crumbs of bread? So Bladys supposed, amused, deafened by their anger and noise.

"Wait," said she; "I have nothing to cast to you now, but the first opportunity that comes I will throw something to you."

Then she turned her face to re-enter the cave. At that same moment a rush of wind drove against her—a draught sweeping through the rock dwelling—and borne on it came voices, confused, menacing. She started.

She had taken a couple of steps within; she stood still; she recoiled a step. Then, thrusting through the narrow doorway by which access to the house was obtained, she saw Luke Onion, his mother, and Abraham Jarrock.

"There she is! Take her! The thief! The thief!" shrieked the old woman; and the hangman, with both hands pushing his mother aside, sprang forward to seize Bladys.

The girl, startled for a moment, was as one paralysed. But she recovered herself and springing through the doorway, threw herself with outspread arms against the rock, and worked her way along the narrow track that led to the old pigeonry.

A little farther was the most ruinous and riskful portion of the path; but she was resolved to attempt this rather than allow herself to be taken. The sleep-walker had been sustained and carried safely to the top of the cliff, why not she?

This thought formed quick as lightning flash, but was instantly brushed away by what she saw, and which produced a spasm of horror.

Looking back at the doorway through which she had just had time to escape, she saw Luke Francis leap through in pursuit, lose his balance, with arms extended battling in the air, and he was precipitated over the edge by the momentum, and disappeared without a cry.

The jackdaws had been given their promised footing.

CHAPTER XXIII. — MEG-A-FOX HOLE

Half-A-Mile from Holy Austin Rock, in the scarp of Kinver Edge, the cliff is precipitous, and has also been utilised from a remote age for the habitation of man. The place is called Meg-a-Fox Hole, and contains a series of caverns connected the one with the other, and somewhat different in construction from the dwellings in Holy Austin Rock.

The face of the cliff is approached by a slope, partly natural, to a large extent composed of the sand thrown out in the construction of the caves, and of the refuse of the dwellers therein from immemorial time. It is probable that an examination of this midden would yield interesting results, and show in successive layers the relics of succeeding races and civilisations that have occupied these troglodyte habitations. This slope is now so much overgrown with masses of tree and enormous hedges of bramble, that the lower portion of the cliff is hidden, and the openings in it are effectually screened, so that the passer-by at the foot of the hill might go before this range of subterranean dwellings without a suspicion of their proximity. No main road, nor even a parish way runs along the bottom; only a cart track in bad condition, little frequented. The place, accordingly, was sufficiently lonely and concealed to invite occupation by those who broke the laws of the land.

Meg-a-Fox Hole is now completely ruinous. Its last tenant left it thirty years ago. Since then it has been sorely disintegrated, in part wantonly destroyed by the mischievous.

Accordingly, although the interior remains unaltered, the exterior has been dismantled and defaced to such an extent as hardly to give an idea of what its appearance was a century ago.

A single doorway cut in the rock gave access to a chain of caves that ran parallel with the face of the cliff, the rock itself, reduced to the thickness of about three feet, interposing between them and the open air; and this face was pierced at intervals with small holes that admitted light, and were so contrived as not to present the appearance of windows. At the beginning of this century, when the cavern was tenanted by a quiet, well-conducted working-man, occasion for concealment was at an end, and he enlarged these openings considerably and put wooden casements into the windows he cut. Since the abandonment of the dwelling and the tearing out of the casements the holes have been further enlarged, and portions of the screening wall wantonly thrown down.

There were, there are still, five chambers. On the left of the portal is an almost circular apartment, nine feet in diameter, opening out of the entrance hall or vestibule, and which may have been used for fuel. The vestibule itself is lighted by a small window on one side of the doorway. From this hall an opening cut in the rock admits to the series of chambers. The first is lighted by a very small hole, that admits but a single ray. Beyond it is the roomy cavern that served as kitchen, furnished with a fireplace scooped out of the screen of living rock, and with a chimney that was carried up in such a manner as to disperse the smoke that issued from it among the bushes. Beyond this kitchen is an extensive hall with an apsidal termination. This was formerly lighted by a mere slit, but it was also furnished with a small door giving access to a narrow shelf that conducted to a flight of steps cut in the face of the cliff, by means of which the downs of Kinver Edge might be reached.

This portion of the habitation was materially altered by the last occupant. He cut large openings in the wall and inserted good windows. All now is in a piteous condition of wreck and ruin. This series of caves has its walls inscribed with names of visitors and tenants. The earliest dated one is that of H. Kindar, Scriptor, Londini, 1700, and the next in antiquity is that of B. Knight, 1749, the great iron-master who founded the family till recently represented by Sir Frederick Winn Knight of Wolverley, on whose land the caverns were. From the extremity of this chain of vaults, it is commonly believed that a passage extends to the river Stour, two miles distant, and animals are reported to have entered the tunnel at the extremity, and to have re-appeared below Kinver Bridge, where there are fissures in the red sandstone from which issue springs of water. That this conception labours under the disadvantage of being almost impossible does not affect the rustic mind. Impossible it almost certainly is, for such a communication would require the tunnel to be carried beneath the bed of the Stour. In reality the passage, now blocked to prevent accidents, extends for half-a-mile to Drakeslowe, a cirque in the sandstone rocks, which is riddled in every direction so as to accommodate the rock to the purpose of human habitation. The dwellings there are almost all in occupation at the present day, and are preferred to those of masonry as warmer in winter and cooler in summer.

At the foot of this amphitheatre of rock houses at Drakeslowe is a modern School Chapel; and on a dark Sunday evening, a singular spectacle is presented by the people emerging from their holes with their lanterns, and descending the stages of the cliff in which they dwell.

We English love to take our holiday by running to the Continent, and fondly imagine that we must cross the Channel to see strange sights and enjoy scenes of beauty. It would be hard to find sweeter, quainter, lovelier spots than may be reached very easily at the point where Shropshire, Worcestershire and Staffordshire join.

Nan Norris was in Meg-a-Fox Hole with the door barred. She was on her knees at the hearth chopping wood for the fire she had kindled, when she was startled by a rap against the door, followed by the scratching as of a cat, and a feeble whistle.

She stood up and listened. The raps were repeated, and a voice called, "Nan, open, will you?"

"Who is there?" she asked, before proceeding to unbar.

"It is I, George Stracey. By Heaven, don't keep me waiting. Open at once, curse your eyes."

Nan proceeded to draw the bars. They were massive irons that ran deep into the rock on each side, and the removal of these was not to be accomplished with speed.

He without became impatient.

"For goodness sake, Nan, bestir yourself. You take matters as leisurely as if there were no danger."

Nan had now removed the lowest bar. There were three in all, and she had previously slipped those above from their places. The door swung open, and Stracey burst in. He was out of breath, and in great agitation.

"You confounded, double-confounded fool!" gasped he, when inside. "What do you mean by keeping me without so long? Had you any one to hide from me? Do you desire to have me swung?"

"George," replied the girl, "you yourself would have cast ugly words at me had I opened too hastily without the sign; and you gave it wrong—you whistled in place of mewing. Nay, I doubt not you would have struck me with your hand, though, by Goles, I'd rather that than have a lick of your rough tongue."

"You fool! don't stand there talking. Fasten up at once with all bars."

He was panting, and white with heat and alarm.

"They are closing in on us," he said. "They have been to my house already, and have ransacked it from attic to cellar; I had a shift to escape. They have found nothing there, for we have all stowed away here; but I am not confident that all is safe in this place. They will go to the Rock Tavern—"

"Where they will find mother deaf and daft. They will get nothing out of her, and find nothing there. The horses are away, and the cow in the underground stable."

"Nan," said Stracey, as he assisted in replanting the bars, "have they a chance of snuffing this lay, think you?"

"I cannot say, George. But they have hold of Jac'mo."

"Curse Jac'mo. Why was he told about it?"

"He was not told anything. But he is no fool. We held from his knowledge all that we were able."

"If he knows, he will lead them here. They have him with them. Has he heard of the underground passage to Drakeslowe?"

"No, George, certainly not. He has never set foot inside Meg-a-Fox Hole; and of the passage none know but yourself and me, and those other two, Hardlow and Kibworth, who are not taken, and who, even if they were, would be torn to pieces before they would peach. You look all a-mort, George."

"I have reason to be. I have had to run for it. Dowse the fire at once, Nan. They mustn't see a glim, nor any reek reach their cursed noses. Not a token must be given that any one is here, and by Moses, they may pass, and miss it altogether."

He did not wait for the girl to do as directed; with his foot he kicked the fuel apart, and spurned the smoking wood about the floor.

"Nan, we must send the blunt down the dolly. If the worst comes about, I must slip down as well."

"And what of me, George?"

"You must stop the earth behind me. It is me they are after, and not you. I'll not be nabbed here, if I can help it. Lend a hand, Nan, with the case; it is confoundedly heavy."

He led into the darkest chamber, where, behind much rubbish heaped against the rock, a chest was concealed. This he extracted from its hiding-place, and with the girl's assistance, drew it into the passage. At that moment a blow crashed against the door, and sent an echo through every chamber.

A voice shouted after it.

"In the King's name—Open!"

Stracey put his finger to his lip and listened then signed to Nan to be speedy with the money chest.

"Deuce take the horsenails (money), the load is heavy as lead. Drag it, and brush the mark over with your foot, as you go along. Quick! Not a minute must be lost. We must have this down the hole, and I will go with it. I will build up, and you toss in the sand, and heap the faggots over the place."

"O George! what is to become of me?"

"You fool! they cannot hurt you. When the blunt and I are gone, what evidence have they got?"

"But, George! let me, I pray you, go along the passage and escape by Drakeslowe with you."

"How can you?" He turned savagely on her with a foul oath. "One must remain behind to cover up the entrance. That cannot be me. You are in no danger."

They had drawn the money chest to the end of the last vault.

At the extremity of this lay a faggot on the ground, and beside it a pile of faggots. Nan quickly removed the prostrate bundle and disclosed a low opening in the rock, level with the floor, so small that a man could enter it only on hands and knees, but within the sides fell apart and the roof rose. On both sides of the entrance were piled pieces of sandstone, by means of which the mouth could be blocked from within; it was further provided that they should be covered with sand. For this purpose a short-handled shovel was secreted behind the stack of fuel. When the loose sand was thrown over the choked mouth of the underground passage, it was effectually hidden.

Into this hole, which Stracey had called the "dolly," he thrust the box of coin, which slid down by its own weight, as within the ground fell rapidly.

Nan was trembling, and her brow was bedewed with sweat. Blows were being rained on the door.

"It will engage them ten minutes to break it in," said Stracey in a whisper; "and by that time this will be built and smothered with sand, and I on my way underground to Drakeslowe."

"O George! I am afraid to stay."

He cursed her.

"Are you going to risk my precious life because of your fears?"

"If only I could escape as well."

"You can do so when you have covered up the mouth. Then go out at the little door—they have not discovered that—and run up the red ladder. What in the devil's name is that?"

A sound, different from that which came from the door, reached their ears and alarmed them. Thud, thud, thud! A dead and muffled sound.

"Nan, run, whilst I build up."

With eager hands Stracey, who was down the hole, built up with stones in order to close the opening of the passage.

Nan sprang back in quivering alarm.

"George! they have found the door too tough. One of them has a pick, and with it he is digging through. Hark!"

A click; then a crash of broken glass.

"There! there!" gasped Nan; "he is widening the window. The rock wall is thin just there. He cannot fail to dig his way in on us directly."

"Nan!" said Stracey, "my life depends on you. Here!" he handed a pistol through the gap that remained unclosed; "take this barking iron and shoot him through head or heart."

"O George!"

"My blood is on your head if you do not. If I am taken, then with my last breath I will curse you, Nan."

"But George!"

"Nan, if you really love me, and have not set your fancy on another, if you are true to me, as you have so often protested, prove it to me now."

She accepted the pistol, cocked it, and ran to the spot where she could see the man, a constable, who was driving his pickaxe in at the window, and ever and anon was shouting encouragingly to his fellows:

"We'll be on them in a minute. I can smell the fire already."

The opening was still too small to admit the passage of a human body, but the man had wrenched out the framework and broken the glass, and was rapidly enlarging the orifice.

"Cease; or I will fire!" cried the girl, presenting her weapon.

The constable stopped, and looked in. He replied in mocking words, that to her were unintelligible. She could see his round head and big body against the sky, but could distinguish no features.

"Desist; or I shoot."

"By heavens, a wench!" he said with a laugh.

She touched the trigger. The pistol exploded. Nan saw the man straighten himself, remain stationary for a moment, then reel over.

A yell of dismay and rage rushed in at the opening—the cry of those who were assaulting the cave—at the sight of their comrade, who fell headlong with a bullet in his forehead.

"That will occupy them for some minutes," laughed Stracey. "Well done, Nan; give me back my pistol."

"I have thrown it away."

"Let it lie. Close up; I am ready."

"George! Kiss me first. Kiss me before we part. It will be for ever. And I know you will soon find someone else. I have killed that man."

"A plague on your sentiment!" answered Stracey, withdrawing his head, without granting her request, and he jammed the last stone into its place.

Then Nan used the shovel with good effect, and in a few minutes had buried the entrance under sand. Not content with this, she cut the binding withy of the faggots, and strewed the contents over the spot. Then she upset the stack upon the loose sticks, and proceeded to cut or untie all their bonds, so that it would not be possible for those who were in pursuit to remove them in bundles, but only piece-meal, stick by stick.

This occupied Nan a considerable time, but she did not for a moment turn her thoughts to her own safety till she had done everything in her power, and in fulfilment of what she regarded as her duty, to effectually disguise the place of Stracey's retreat.

The men outside had again got to work, and were redoubling their efforts to effect an entrance. Of them, however, none would venture at the window, lest he should be picked off in the same manner as his fellow.

The door was too strongly barred to be driven in; but by means of a pick-axe the assailants were cutting through the sandstone outside so as to disengage the frame of the door, and enable them to draw it outwards.

In a quarter of an hour this was effected. The heavy oak door, no longer held in place by a rebate of stone, fell forward with a crash, and the constables withdrew the now useless bars, and burst into the cavern with a shout.

Nan had in the meantime shut and fastened the door of communication with the inner chamber; this impediment could not detain them long, but it would furnish her with sufficient time to effect her escape by the postern, and to run up the ladder, cut in the face of the cliff, which communicated with the top of the Edge and the open downs, over which she might fly, and find concealment in nooks known only to a few.

To this door she sped. It was locked. She put her hands to her temples. Her brain was whirling. Where was the key? She felt in her pocket. She turned herself on all sides. Oh! where was the key?

Then with horror and despair she recalled where it was, and knew that it was beyond her reach. George Stracey alone retained possession of the key, so that he might obtain admission to Meg-a-Fox Hole whenever he pleased. That key he ever carried about his person.

That key he had with him, when he bade her escape by the postern door. Yet he had not given it her. She had not thought to ask for it. Had he purposely carried it away with him and left her to her fate, knowing that he could have saved her had he willed?

No! no! no! In her true generous heart she repelled this thought; nevertheless a vein of gall broke in her heart as she allowed that he, in his supreme solicitude about his own safety, had not given sufficient thought to her to remember that he carried with him the means of affording her the opportunity of escape.

Nan sank on the little rock-hewn bench, laid her face in her hands and wept.

Next minute rude hands were on her, and she heard shouts of—"Where is Stracey? What have you done with him?"

"He is not here," answered Nan, recovering composure.

"Who then shot Thomson?" was asked.

"I did that. Yonder lies the pistol on the floor."

"Secure her," said the magistrate, who had entered. "She has killed an officer of the Crown whilst in discharge of his duty."

"By heaven!" exclaimed a constable, "it is well that Luke Hangman is in Kinver, to measure her for the cravat."

CHAPTER XXIV. — AT THE ROCK FOOT

Erect, rigid, stood Mother Onion beside the corpse of her son extended at the foot of Holy Austin Rock. Her face was livid, strained and knotted in muscle with the cramp of excitement and resentment that held her soul. Her harsh features were strongly illumined by the setting sun. They seemed to be chiselled out of marble—an orange marble—not moulded in flesh, and chiselled by an unskilful workman. But her eyes gleamed with lightning flashes.

Luke Hangman lay extended his length at her feet, on his back, his arms outspread, and his mouth half-open. That he was dead could not for a moment be doubted, nor did his mother entertain a hope to the contrary.

There surged up in her heart a rage against Bladys, to whom she attributed his death, like the bore in the Severn—it rolled through her, invading every sense, flushing her every vein.

A ring of spectators had formed. Jarrock had come down from the rock holding Bladys by the arm to prevent her from attempting escape.

The inhabitants of the occupied prong of sandstone issued from their burrows. Scarce a denizen was left behind. Even a half-paralysed woman had scrambled from her bed, drawn herself to the verge of the cliff, and hung her head, benimbed with the frills of a great night-cap, over the edge, looking down on what took place below, unwilling to miss seeing and hearing whatever might occur. Children, unable to thrust themselves in between their elders, climbed portions of the rock to overtop them, or ensconced themselves high aloft in the forks of over-hanging Scotch pines. Holy Austin, who had been at a little distance, hurried up with two companions, with whom he had been in conversation. One was the Evening Lecturer and the other Squire Folliot. Seeing Bladys held by the executioner's assistant, he at once went to him, and demanded her release.

This gave fresh occasion for the excitement of the bereaved woman. With extended hand and outstretched finger she pointed to Bladys.

"See! See!" she shrieked; "that is the murderess. I give her in charge. I accuse her. She thrust my son, her husband, over the precipice. She killed him. Last week we burnt a woman at Shrewsbury for poisoning her husband. Now we shall have another execution."

Gasping for breath, she placed one hand on her bosom, whilst still indicating Bladys with the other.

"That woman at Shrewsbury we strangled at the stake before the flame touched her. But she, she shall burn and feel all the anguish of the fire. The law allows it. The law makes no provision for strangling. That is the pure grace of the executioner. It is as he wills it. He may let her dance in the fire if it pleases him. Abraham Jarrock will be the hangman now; and he will do as I say."

"Nay; reckon not on me," called Jarrock.

Now the old schoolmaster stood forward.

"Woman," said he, in authoritative tones, "your sorrow has perverted your reason. Satis eloquentiæ sapientiæ parum. We respect and we pity you. Let us now raise and bear away the dead man to Kinver, where an inquest will be held on his death."

"He shall not be removed. Here he lies, and here stand I. Here he stays till I am assured that she who killed him is to be conveyed to gaol. Where is a constable? Where is a Justice of Peace?"

"This is arrant folly," said Holy Austin. "But that you are to be commiserated, we would not endure it."

"Not endure it! It is truth. I will swear it. Where is a constable? Bring me a justice here, and I will take oath."

"Here is a magistrate—Squire Folliot."

"Let him draw nigh. Let him swear me!" screamed the frantic woman.

Then, as someone stooped to raise the body, she thrust him fiercely away.

"No! none shall touch him. As he goes to burial so shall the murderess go to the stake—earth to earth here," pointing to her son, "and ashes to ashes there," indicating Bladys. "I will throw myself down. I will clasp him with my arms. None shall separate us till I know that justice will be done him and me, and that this murderess will be conveyed to gaol."

Then an elderly, stout gentleman, in drab smalls and gaiters, thrust his way through the crowd.

"I am a magistrate, madam, and if you can show real cause against that young person, I shall not be slack in performing my duty. Has anyone a New Testament here?"

"I have one, sir," answered the Evening Lecturer, extending a book through the ring of spectators. Mr Folliot at once administered the oath.

The fierce, resentful woman rapidly proceeded with her declaration and denunciation.

"So help me God, I saw her when we came in, Abraham and I, into her cave. She stood in the farther doorway. And when Luke went to her, with both hands she thrust him over the edge down the cliff. I saw it with both eyes. So help me God, Amen."

"Now look here," said the justice, "this is a serious allegation. Where is this same Abraham you mention?"

"I am here, sir; Abraham Jarrock is my name."

"Come forward and take oath."

"I cannot swear to what she says."

"Take oath as to what you actually witnessed."

"I did not see the girl thrust him over. She went through the door and the master ran after her, and as he knew nothing of the precipice beyond, fell headlong down unaided. He was quite capable of doing so without assistance."

"You say that? You lie!" shrieked the woman. "You were not looking. I have sworn. Take her away; handcuff her! Carry her to prison. It was her husband she killed. She shall not end on the gallows, she shall be burned alive."

"Silence, woman," said the magistrate. "The assistant, Abraham Jarrock, contradicts your statement. There are other witnesses."

"I am one, your worship!" said Holy Austin, stepping through the ring and taking his place by the corpse over against the woman. "Hand me the book. I, also, have something to say, and I will speak before this assembly."

"Stay awhile," said the justice. "Whom have we here?"

Mr Folliot looked over the heads of the people, and saw a gentleman on horseback advancing, followed by several men, some bearing a hurdle on which lay a body, and two conducting a woman who was handcuffed.

The throng about the dead executioner and his mother loosened; its texture resolved itself into an open web. Attention was for a moment diverted by this new event, as yet not understood, but stimulating enquiry.

Then the magistrate called:

"Mr Homfray! Will you be good enough to come here? We shall be glad of your presence and assistance."

The gentleman addressed alighted from his horse, the constables attending him approached. Hasty questions were put, and as hastily answered. The party just arrived was the posse which had broken into Meg-a-Fox Hole, and it was conveying the dead constable to the village and Nan to the lock-up.

"Mr Homfray," said Justice Folliot, "I particularly desire your presence here. Will you kindly step forward?" Turning to Mother Onion he said, "There are now two magistrates present, and this charge of yours shall be impartially considered. But let me caution you, madam; you are not in a condition now to speak without a passion that clouds your vision. Be advised by me and say no more."

"I will speak. I am on my oath. I insist on being heard. I will repeat all again."

"I will briefly tell my brother magistrate what you have said, and what is the accusation you make."

"That girl yonder, as I hear, has killed a man," cried Mrs Onion, pointing to Nan, "and she is under arrest. Why should this other go free, when she has murdered my son? I insist, I will repeat my charge."

This she did with as great volubility and vehemence as before.

"Now it is my turn to speak," said Holy Austin. He kissed the book. "I am glad to have occasion, as there is much to be said which I desire should be heard by all."

"Speak on, Knobbler!" said Justice Folliot.

"It is my desire," said the old man, "to say a word touching the marriage. Mrs Onion declares that the case is one of petty treason—that the murder, if murder it be, was committed on the body of Luke Francis Onion by his lawful wife. Now, I deny that deceased was her husband. You are all aware that the father of Stewponey Bladys set her as a prize to be contended for at bowls. This match was got up at the instigation of some of the bloods and bucks of the neighbourhood. At that time Luke Francis Onion, the public executioner of the counties of Shropshire and Staffordshire, was tarrying at the Stewponey Inn, not under his proper name, but under that of Francis. None suspected him to be the hangman, or none would have associated with him. This man won in the game of bowls, and claimed the prize. Unhappily, our vicar, perhaps over-persuaded by a gentleman I do not see here perhaps believing that as the Chapel of Stourton Castle is extra-parochial, any sort of ceremony may be performed there with impunity, even to the worship of Baal, was induced to give his aid. The scene in the Chapel was a scandal to religion. The House of God was invaded by a rabble of gentlemen-blackguards—"

"Come, come, Knobbler, I cannot allow this," said Folliot.

"I beg pardon, your worship; but unhappily, as you well know, our district harbours a number of gentlemen by birth and position who are the leaders in all that is degrading—in cock-fighting, Sabbath-breaking, cudgelling, dicing, swearing, and blasphemy. I will not say more of that outrage on religion, the pretended marriage, than that it lacks all those elements which go to make it legal. It is not registered in the parish books, there is no record of it, as there would have been had it been a proper and legal function. Our vicar probably was ashamed of his part in the affair, and did no more than he conceived himself engaged to do by a promise wrung from him by a certain person I will not name. I presume that a marriage performed without banns, or without licence, in an unauthorised place, and unrecorded in the register—one, moreover, in which the one party—the bride—refused to give any promise and consent—is no marriage in the sight of God or in the eye of the law. Consequently, the charge of petty treason breaks down.

"Now, as to the next point. There was no murder committed. That this gentlewoman should have suffered a terrible loss makes us all compassionate her. But the sense of commiseration is swallowed up in indignation when we hear her give false evidence, and swear to what is demonstrably a lie, in order that she may glut her hate upon the unhappy girl who has for too long been misunderstood, misrepresented, and misused. Interest magistratûs tueri bonos, animadvertere in malos.

"May it please your worships, one word further. , whom this gentlewoman accuses of having thrust the deceased over the rock with both hands, was not where represented by Mrs Onion. She was not within reach of him when he fell. Outside the western door is a narrow shelf that led to a pigeonry. I had quitted the rock some ten minutes before the event of the fall of Luke Hangman, an event we all deplore. I had gone to the front of the rock and had met the Evening Lecturer, and with him walked on the heath, and lit upon Squire Folliot. We happened to speak of the presentation of our vicar to the bishop on account of his irregularities, and I then informed the Squire and the Lecturer that the young person who had been so irregularly married was taken under my protection and was in the Rock. I turned, as did also they, and I pointed to the opening from her dwelling, and at that moment we all three—that is to say, I, and I doubt not the gentlemen will say the same—saw her issue forth, and creep along the ledge till she was fully two arms' length from the doorway. Then we all three—that is to say, I—saw a man—who he was I knew not then, leap through the opening and fall down the cliff, carried over by his own weight. If she had touched him I should have seen it, but touch him she could not and did not. She was standing with both arms spread, clinging with her hands to the surface of the rock. This is what I have to say. The Rev. Mr Wittinslow, the Lecturer, and Squire Folliot will confirm my statement."

Mrs Onion was staggered, but she promptly rallied.

"I charge her," she said hoarsely, "I charge her with having robbed me of jewels worth over a thousand pounds."

"Hearken to me, madam," said Mr Folliot, gravely. "To my certain knowledge you have already perjured yourself. You have endeavoured to injure a perfectly innocent young girl. My own eyes have assured me of that. If my brother justice desires it, I am ready to be put on oath. No sooner does one monstrous charge break down than you trump up another, equally preposterous I doubt not. We are ready to believe that grief at the loss of your son has disturbed your mind, and that you are not responsible for what you say. But take care of yourself. You are now the only person menaced, for you have rendered yourself liable to a warrant issued against you for perjury; and, by Heaven, if we have another word on this matter of poor Stewponey, we will deal with you in such manner as you will not relish."

Turning aside, he muttered: "She is a malignant, wicked old cat!" Then to some of the men who stood by he said, curtly, "Remove the corpse."

Abraham Jarrock pushed to the foreground, and thrusting his sour face close to the stupefied mother, said sneeringly:

"Dost desire to know who killed the master? It was your own self. He had no fancy to go to the Rock. He had tasted quite sufficient of the sours of matrimony. He told me himself on the way that he should not bring back his wife, and that he went solely in order to humour you. So it was you who drove him to it, you who threw him down, you who broke his neck, you who have opened the way to me to become hangman-in-chief. I thank you for it. I shall ask for my appointment and shall get it. Go back to Shrewsbury, pack up your duds at the Gate House and sheer off."

CHAPTER XXV. — NAN, FAREWELL!

Alas for Nan! There was little to be hoped for when her case came on for trial.

Bladys spoke to Holy Austin about her. The old man had heard from his nephew. The jewels were the property of Bladys. The Crown would not press its claim. Consequently she would have money by the sale, and her first desire was that whatever was necessary should be done for Nan Norris.

The old schoolmaster shook his head; a counsel had already been engaged, and had visited Nan in prison, and had concerted with her a line of defence. But the Knobbler was not sanguine.

It was with tears in her eyes that Bladys entered the prison at Stafford to visit her friend. She found Nan at the little window of her cell, looking up at the flying clouds. The sun shone in when a cloud was withdrawn from the disc, and then her pleasant countenance was glorified, and a smile and a dimple formed on lip and in cheek, as her changeful mood assumed a hopeful complexion, with the flash of light upon it Next moment a cloud drifted across the orb, and then, as Nan's face was overshadowed, its expression also became despondent. The tears filled her eyes as the rain filled the passing mass of vapour.

Her hands lay in her lap, but she could not keep them in repose. She plucked at her gown incessantly; then, as Bladys entered, she started up, ran to her, and in her impulsive way said:

"Bla, see this; my fingers have been picking at threads. That is ever a bad sign, mother says, and is a sure token of death."

There was something in the girl's handsome face that was inexpressibly engaging. The dark eye of old, twinkling with humour or melting with kindliness, had in it now a soft appealing gleam. Her dimpled cheek, ready to flush with passion, was now somewhat pale. The mobile lips that were always inclined to smile good-humouredly were now tremulous with sorrow. There was ever in the girl strength as well as good nature, and where her heart was engaged she could be tough as steel. And this strength did not desert her now. If the tears rose readily to Nan's eyes and the glow of anger to her cheek the mood quickly changed, and then there shone a rainbow in her eyes—a promise of fine weather.

Bladys did not dare to extend to the poor creature hopes that were almost certain to be blasted, and to represent her case as lighter than it really was. The girl frankly admitted that she had fired at and shot the constable. Her plea was that he was breaking into her habitation, and that she had a right to defend herself. She was making Meg-a-Fox Hole ready, as her mother thought of giving up the Rock Tavern and of removing thither. When the attack was made she was alarmed. She knew not who the assailants were. They might have been housebreakers, murderers. She defended herself and her goods as well as she was able. She had no more to say than that any girl under like provocation, in deadly fear for herself, would have been justified in defending herself. Such was the line of defence agreed upon; but Nan herself laughed over it to Bladys. It was not likely to be accepted. It was too well established that Nan and her mother were in league with the gang of highwaymen infesting the country. The Savoyard was able to give evidence to this effect, and further proof was not wanting.

There was no evidence that the Norris family purposed leaving the tavern; there was good proof that the series of caves called Meg-a-Fox Hole was used as a place of concealment for stolen goods, and it was ostensibly held by Mother Norris, who paid for it a trifling acknowledgment to the Lord of the Manor.

"O Bla! Bla!" sobbed Nan, clinging to her visitor, "I shall know the worst very soon. Come and see me afterwards. Do not forsake me. George, I know, can't come. He is having a bad time of it hiding about. I'd have been told if he had been nabbed. Well, they'll tire of hunting after him, and if he'll keep moving about from one ken to another for a week or two longer he may get off. Mother has been here to see me. Holy Austin brought her. I am sure it gave him trouble to persuade her. She is that terrible afraid of gaols and gallows and all that sort of thing, that she won't come near a court o' law or a prison. But, anyhow, she did come, and when she was here she made it bad for me. She was that inquisitive and curious, axing me a score of questions about—But there, I'll say nothing of that, even to you, my dear. Bla, sit here by me on my bed. I want to tell you something."

She took hold of the hand of Bladys, and began to stroke it. "I'm not, after all, so sorry that I am about to die."

"O Nan!"

"It is true. You do not know all; I will tell you. You remember when you was to be bowled for, when George said he would play, I began to hate you then. I was miserable. But I had a sort of tiff about it with George, and he gave up the notion: I think he was a bit afraid of me. Mother and I knew so much. We knew everything, and could blow the whole concern. If mother or I turned cat-in-the-pan, where would the Captain be? Where would—but I will name no names. He and the other gentlemen have been forced to trust us, and never, never have we acted dishonourable by 'em. George and I were woundy friendly. But he is of a changeable complexion and terribly humoursome. I've seen it coming on for some while, and very miserable it has made me. He's been getting tired of me, and my life has just been one running festering sore. It has been all pain and no happiness all through this. Whether he has set his fancy on some other doxie, I can't tell. He's been clever enough not to allow me to know, but he has not been for some time to me what he once was, and it is my conviction, Bla, that but for fear of offending me, and so making me ready to peach, he'd have shaken me off two months agone."

Nan sobbed convulsively. She squeezed the hand of Bladys and held it to her bosom, then kissed it.

"Well, it had come to this. I found him every day trying to undo one tie and then another that bound us together, and to me the misery was becoming more than I could bear. Bla, that is one reason why I am ready to die. To live on, deserted by him, to be nothing more to him, to know that his heart belonged to another, I could not bear it. O Bla!" she loosed her hold on Bladys, and flung herself on the bed with her face down and beat the counterpane with her hands, "I could not bear it. I would rather die than go through it."

Recovering herself, she sat up again and continued:

"But that is not all. There is worse behind. I should not have rested by day or by night. I'd have been ever looking who she was that had stolen him away from me. And then, if I had discovered—and from a jealous, resentful and wretched woman nothing of that kind can be hid for long—then, Bla, darling, I'd have become that wicked, I'd have killed her. Mother would have lent a hand, and been pleased to do so. Lor' bless y', she thinks no more of that sort of thing than of poisoning rats. She is a clever woman is mother, and knows the herbs, like any other wise woman. It has been in the family. Her mother was just the same. But there now, I'm off to something else, and time is flying. Bla! think of that. If I'd got out, and lived, and was unhappy with having lost George, I might have come to be a real wicked murderess. I would have done it with hate in my heart, and a wish for revenge.

"As to the poor chap I shot, by Goles, I bore him no malice; I could not see who it was, and I did my duty in shooting him. George bade me fire. I did it to save him. If I had not blazed at him, in another minute he'd have been in the cave, and all the others after him. There is just this comfort to me," she wiped her eyes, "that George can't think unkindly of me, though there have been brushes between us sometimes. One or other—it had come to that. He or I must go to feed the crows, so, of course, there was no choice for me. Now, look you here, and listen and attend to what I say. Mother, she'll be in a pretty take-on about me. She puts it all down to George, and I want you to do me a favour. It is the last in the world that you can."

"I will do anything that I can for you, dear Nan!"

"I know you will," with another gush of affection. "You are the only real friend I have, or ever have had—all but George, and he is not true. But for all that, I'm sorry not to say good-bye to him. No, Bla! I'm glad I am going; it is all for the best, and I feel that in my heart o' hearts. George will not forget that he escaped by means of me."

"But what is it that you desire me to do for you, Nan?"

"There now, I am wandering again. I am a fool, as George was never tired of telling me. I didn't like it then, but I dare be sworn he was right. It is just this—Do everything you can to find him."

"Whom, Nan?"

"George, of course. There is no other he to me."

"That will be difficult if he is in hiding."

"I know it will be. Perhaps if all other means fail, you may learn about him from my mother; but find him, if you can, before she sees him. When you have discovered him, then"—she drew the ear of Bladys to her lips and whispered, "bid him never eat a bit of food or take a sup of drink from my mother. Do you understand? Tell him that from me. When I am swung, then I shall know nothing of how he goes on with other girls. I shan't mind, if he keeps one kind thought of Nan in his heart. Tell him," she whispered again, trembling with eagerness as she spoke, "tell him from me never to accept a bit or drop from mother. Hark! there they come! I know it is to take me into Court. God be wi' ye, Bla. Kiss me again. You will not forget my message? Give my love to George."

"Farewell, Nan!"

Mother Norris was sitting by the fire, smoking a short pipe, and looking dreamily into the glow. A few days had sufficed to olden her by as many years. The anxiety under which she had laboured when her house had been searched, and her distress about Nan, had aged her vastly. Her back was more bent, her face more haggard, her hair greyer and more dishevelled, and her eyes more dazed.

She had seen her daughter. The assizes at Stafford had followed so speedily after those at Shrewsbury that Nan's imprisonment had been brief, and only a few weeks had intervened, no more, between the death of the constable and her execution.

Now the old woman was full of concern for herself and her future. In her old age, with her natural selfishness, she grieved for the loss of her daughter mainly as it affected her own comfort. She was afraid that she would be driven out of her old home. But even if allowed to continue there, how could she conduct the business of the house unassisted? To engage a helper when she was in such a feeble condition was to put everything into the hands of the assistant. She sat blinking and puffing over the embers, with one brown, lean hand on each knee, endeavouring to discover some expedient for making the rest of her life independent and comfortable, and could find none.

Then she was startled by a rap, followed by a scratching at the door. She called in reply, and the door was partially opened. A face looked in, peered into every corner, and then a body followed.

"Ah, George! My darling, my honey-man!" croaked the old woman. "Come in; I am alone. You are safe here. But I've had them rumpling the place up twice."

Stracey shut and bolted the door after him. If the events of the past weeks had worn and oldened the woman, they had told with even greater effect on the man. He was pale to ghastliness, had lost flesh, his swagger had given way to nervousness, and his very garments had partaken in his deterioration. They were soiled and ragged. He threw himself into a chair by the hearth and cowered by the fire.

"It has come to this," said he, "that I'm pretty nigh done for. They are stopping every earth, and I have had to run from one ken to another, and have never known where I was safe. I've had to sleep in ditches and under trees, been soaked by rains and shivered by frosts. I haven't had a proper bite of food since I last saw you. By Heaven, I must eat, and I'll throw myself on a doss (bed) to-night if I have to swing for it. But I won't be caught; they are hunting in another quarter now. I can't endure this much longer; I'll shift to Wales."

"Why have you come here?" said Mrs Norris, holding the pipe in her hand, and eyeing him with a singular expression in her leathery face. He was too weary, hungry, miserable, to observe of her countenance.

"Why have I come?" said he impatiently; "you have potatoes, bacon; that is why. Bring me rye bread— anything. I am sick for want of proper meat and sleep."

"I've no taters in the house, and not a bit of bacon for the last fortnight. But I'll bring you a drop of cat-water (gin), and warm you some porridge with onions."

"Anything that is hot. I'm starved. Am I safe here?"

"How can I say? This is a pot-house, and folk come in for a drop at all hours. If they find the door locked and barred they'll smell something, and go into Kinver and lay an information."

"Let me have the inner room. Then if anyone should enter you can keep 'em in the kitchen as usual; and they'll know nothing of my being under this roof. But when I've eaten and warmed me at the fire I'll just throw myself on the doss."

He went to the door of communication and looked into the dark and unoccupied chamber.

"I'll not be in yonder, in cold and blackness, I've been a fortnight and more without seeing or smelling a fire. I'm starving for warmth and dryth, as I am for proper food. See—my clothing—rags they be; you can almost wring the water out of them."

"I'll kindle the fire in yonder," said Mrs Norris; "and then if any one comes to the door you can step in there. I can't refuse to open."

"I know that; I would not have come here but that I have nowhere else whither I can run. Look at my hand, how it shakes. That is with cold and fasting and being hounded about, and never sure whether I shan't be nabbed, and in the end crapped."

"My fell (daughter) has been that," said the hostess, leaning over Stracey and looking into his face with inquiry in her eyes.

He rubbed his hands together and extended them over the fire again, but did not respond to the remark.

"Do you know that?" asked Mother Norris. "She's turned off and done for. Last Tuesday it was. What I am to do without her I can't think. I always reckoned that you'd make a tavern sign, but I never reckoned that my Nan would be swung up. Captain, how came that about? I'd like to know. You was with her in Meg-a-Fox Hole. Couldn't you have got her off?"

"You hell-hag! I had as much as I could do to save myself."

"And the dust—what became of that? I know it was got away. How did you manage to carry that away and leave my Nan behind? I know you got off with the blunt, for they turned over everything in the cave and did not find it."

"Yes, yes; I thrust it down the dolly!"

"Then why did you leave Nan behind? She was more to me than my share of the dust. She ought not to have been lagged when you were there to help her."

With an oath George Stracey turned on the old woman and bade her get the fire lighted in the farther room and prepare food for him.

She said not another word, but hobbled into the adjoining apartment, and remained there for some minutes. Presently she returned to take a shovel-full of red-hot embers from the kitchen hearth, with which to kindle the fire in the grate of the inner chamber. As she stopped and with a hook drew the ashes into the shovel she leered up into the face of the highwayman and said:

"Ah! Captain, honey! What are you thinking and grieving over? No more games on the main toby (highway)? Or is it for Nan? Poor, poor Nan."

The man stamped and set his teeth.

"Have I not enough to worry me without you snapping at me?"

"Just so she used to sit, looking into the glow," continued the hag, undeterred; "with her it was nought but George this and George that; ay, ay, it was all George with her. I've seen her fret her heart out, there on that stool, when she fancied you was ceasing to care for her, and had took up with some other jorner."

"Get me something to eat. Don't you know I'm perished for food?" exclaimed Stracey, with an impatient action of the hand that made the woman wince, as she thought he was about to strike her.

She obeyed, her face wreathed with a smile more hideous than a scowl.

After a few minutes she returned, and said in a muffled voice, "Everything is ready."

"Not more ready than am I," said the highwayman, rising stiffly. "Zounds! I've had nothing baken and hot from the fire between my teeth for many days; nought but raw turnips or a handful of dry corn."

He went into the adjoining room and threw the door back after him.

The chamber he entered was lighted by a dancing fire of sticks, in joyful contrast to the dull red fire over which he had crouched in the kitchen, and which had been reduced in volume by the red-hot embers taken to supply the other grate.

Stracey had not left the kitchen many minutes before steps were heard approaching; then a hand was laid on the latch and an attempt was made to open the door.

"Who is there?" asked Mother Norris.

"Come—open. A public-house should never be fast shut," was the reply.

"Eh! but I am lone and old now."

"We will not harm you. Unbar."

"But who are you? There be more than one."

"Ay, to be sure there be. Crispin Ravenhill and Stewponey Bla. You're not afraid of us?"

At the door of communication between the inner room and the kitchen, appeared Stracey, signalling to the old woman. But she paid no attention to him, and withdrew the bar.

"Come in, and welcome," she said. "There be so many wicked men about, that I'm forced, when feeling timorsome of nights, to bolt my door. What are you two about, wandering in the wind and rain and darkness?"

"We have made this journey to see you," answered the young man in the doorway. "It has been the wish of Bladys, and I am but now returned from London town."

"Come to the fire. Sit you down," said the hag.

"We shall not remain over ten minutes," said Crispin. "We must return to the Rock and Kinver."

He strode to the hearth and stood there.

A strip of gold, the reflection from the fire in the farther apartment, through the gap made by the door being ajar, was painted from ceiling to floor, on the wall—a ribbon of flickering gold leaf.

The haste with which Mrs Norris had undone the front door, had prevented Stracey from shutting that into the room where he was.

"You have a fire in yonder," said Ravenhill. "Is there anyone there?"

"No—no—no one," answered the old woman. "I have kindled a faggot, as the night was damp and the room smelled mouldy, like a church vault."

Then Bladys took the hand of Mrs Norris, and said in a shaking voice:

"Mother, I have come to say a word to you about her whom we have lost—whom I loved as well as you."

"Ay! ay!" replied the crone. "She was a good wench, and was very fond of you. She loved me too, although I was rough with her at times. She was my own flesh and blood, and although I say it, she was a good wench; and I take it kindly of you to come and speak to me of her. That's more than do some as ought to." Her tone suddenly altered. "She would ha' done better to have dashed a kettle o' scalding water in a face I could put a name to, than to have cast eyes of love on it."

"As you say," spoke Bladys in feeling tones, "she was good and true, and we will remember her as such. I ever shall—to me she was loving."

"That's certain," exclaimed the old woman, casting a sidelong glance at the door that was ajar. "And if right had been done by such as I know of, she'd have been here to-night to welcome you, and would not have got her head into a horse's nightcap."

She stooped over the fire, and put the miserable embers together and muttered, "Somebody might have saved her had he chose."

"Do not entertain these notions," said Bladys. "What has happened is past recall."

"True, but, Stewponey Bla, I saw my Nan before she died. Holy Austin took me to her, or I never should have mustered up courage to go. She was woundy shy of speaking to me, but I probed her well wi' questions, and when she turned stiff and wouldn't give me a reply, then I sullied the truth. Yes, yes, the cravat was but to her neck that should have been fitted to the throat of another."

It was in vain for Bladys to get the old woman to speak of her daughter in any other light. She harboured the conviction that a wrong had been done to her and Nan, and was bitter in heart with resentment against the offender, whom, however, she would not name. Bladys accordingly turned to another matter.

"Mother," she said, "for all that Nan was to me, for the love that I bore her, I wish to do something for you. I know that you are poor, very poor, and now, in your old age, companion-less and helpless. It is my wish and intention, along with Crispin, who—who will soon be my husband, to do something for you."

"What can you do?" asked the old woman sharply.

"We will allow you a crown every week, on which you may be able to obtain little comforts."

The old woman laughed.

"You must have the money before you can give it."

"We have it," answered Bladys. "I may tell you that we have come in for a large sum of money—large, that is, for us."

"A large sum—When? How?" greedily queried the beldame. "Have you it about you now? Show it me."

"No, Mother Norris, I have none of it about me now. Crispin is going to expend it in barges on the canal. We shall have enough over with which to assist you. You shall receive a crown every week, from Holy Austin if we are away. And if at any time you should need more we shall not refuse further help, for dear Nan's sake."

"I'd like to know how you came by that money," said the hag meditatively. "Not from Holy Austin—he has none. Not from your father—he wants it all for the dressing-up of his new jorner. Not from Luke Hangman or his mother—for I've heard say that you never was his wife, and so couldn't claim aught when he was dead."

"I have my secrets," said Bladys, with a smile, "even from you."

"There is one thing, further, and then we must be gone," said Crispin. "Where is Captain Stracey?"

"Where is George Stracey?" repeated the old woman, slowly, musingly. "Oh! you desire to know?"

"Yes, Bla does."

Then Bladys, standing near the hearth, saw in the streak of flickering gold reflected on the wall before her, the shadow of a hand with a crooked forefinger, making a sign of caution. With an exclamation of astonishment she turned on her heels, and cried, "He is here!"

At the same moment Crispin sprang at the door and drove it open, and saw Stracey standing with spanned pistol presented at him.

"Back!" shouted the highwayman, and snapped the lock. No discharge followed; the priming was wet. With a curse Stracey turned the weapon in his hand and said:

"Come on if you dare. I'll sell my life dearly."

"I have no desire to touch you, or to have anything to do with you," said Ravenhill coolly.

"Then why ask Mother Norris to betray me?"

"I asked her where you were, because she who is soon to become my wife brings you a message from poor Nan."

Bladys advanced into the room.

"Captain," said she, "have no fears for yourself, no hurt will come to you through us. Nan loved you too dearly for me not to wish you well. For her sake I would screen you. But I can do nothing in that way. Nan made me promise that I would give you a message from her—one I was to communicate to no ear save yours."

"What is it?" he asked, sullenly and suspiciously.

"I must speak it to you alone. Crispin will leave the room, go into the kitchen, and suffer us to be together for a moment."

Ravenhill withdrew and shut the door.

"Come, what is it?"

"It really is not much," answered Bladys; "only this. Nan said, 'Tell George Stracey on no account to touch food or drink prepared for him by my mother.'"

The man staggered back, turned livid, his eyes fell; he put his hand through his hair and whispered—he could not speak—"It is too late! Look!" and he pointed to an empty bowl on the table.

Then his paralysing terror instantly gave way, and in a transport of fury and resentment he dashed past Bladys, tore open the door, and would have fallen on Mother Norris and beaten out her brains with his fists had not Ravenhill intervened and repelled him.

"She has poisoned me!" he yelled; the sweat bursting, almost spouting, from his lips and brow. "I know it—I feel it. Why did I ever come here?"

Unable to reach her he ran back into the room he had left, picked up the pistol that had fallen from his hand in the first access of horror, again cocked it, and once more attempted to discharge it, this time aiming at the hag. Again the weapon refused to fire, and he threw it at her, but missed.

"She has poisoned me—with her cursed drie," he gasped; then suddenly turned and fled the house.

The old woman, hugging her knee, seated by the fire, broke into convulsions of harsh laughter.

"Drie, is it! Accursed drie! Oh, Captain George—Captain Stracey—who could have thought that he who has been the terror of travellers, has defied the law and slipped the noose, should find his death in a porridge bowl!"

"Come from this place," cried Ravenhill, drawing Bladys to him. "Leave the miserable creature to herself. This is no place for you."

He led her from the Rock Tavern.

The rain had ceased, the clouds had parted, the stars shone clear. Jupiter as a silver lamp stood above. From beyond the Stour sounded soft and sweet the warble of a flute; a lad was practising outside his cottage door.

"Bladys!" said Crispin, and he drew the shaking, trembling girl closer to his side, "another month and then we leave Kinver, and put behind us thoughts that are painful and the memory of many horrors, and in the new home in which you will be known as Bladys Ravenhill a new and happy story will begin, full of love and joy and peace, and the old tale of Stewponey Bla, into which entered so much of distress, shame, and sorrow, will be closed—ay, and forgotten."

APPENDIX. — BURNING FOR PETTY TREASON

IN 1769 Susannah Lott was burned for the murder of her husband, at Canterbury, and Benjamin Buss, her paramour, was hanged for participation in the crime.

Catherine Hayes was burned alive in 1726. Her son, Billings, who had assisted her in the murder of her husband, was hung. "An iron chain was put round her body, with which she was fixed to a stake near the gallows." On these occasions, when women were hanged for petty treason, it was customary to strangle them, by means of a rope passed round the neck, and pulled by the executioner, so that they were dead before the flames reached the body. But this woman was literally burnt alive: for the executioner letting go the rope sooner than usual, in consequence of the flames reaching his hands, the fire burnt fiercely round her, and the spectators beheld her pushing away the faggots, while she rent the air with her cries and lamentations. Other faggots were instantly thrown on her; but she survived amidst the flames for a considerable time, and her body was not reduced perfectly to ashes in less than three hours.— "Chronicles of Crime, or the New Newgate Calendar." G. C. Pelham, June 1840.

"From a prison chaplain's MS. private prayer-book I copy, that in 1732 a woman was hanged, taken down while the body was warm, and then burnt; and this is recorded as if the process were usual, and as if women were not burnt alive then. J. HODGSON."

A poor girl of fifteen was burnt at Heavitree, near Exeter, on July 29, 1782, for poisoning her master, Richard Jarvis, with arsenic. A broadside ballad was circulated among the crowd who witnessed the execution, of which this is the last verse:—

"When to the fatal stake I come
And dissipate in flame.
Let all be warn'd by my sad doom.
To shun my sin and shame.
May I thus expiate my crime.
And whilst I undergo
The fiery trial here on earth.
Escape the flames below."

A woman was burnt at Winchester in 1783. A writer in "Notes and Queries," June 1, 1850, says:

"A gentleman lately deceased told me the circumstances (of a case in 1789) minutely. I think that he had been at the trial, but I know that he was at the execution, and saw the wretched woman fixed to the stake, fire put to the faggots, and her body burnt. But I know two persons still alive who were present at her execution, and I endeavoured in 1848 to ascertain from one of them the date of the event. I made a note of his answer, which was to this effect: I can't recollect the year, but I remember the circumstance well. It was about sixty-five years ago. I was there along with the crowd. I sat on my father's shoulder, and saw them burn her... They fixed her neck by a noose to the stake, and then set fire to the faggots and burnt her."

This woman was Christiana Murphy, alias Budman, convicted of coining. She was stood on a stool, and the stool was removed from under her just before fire was put to the faggots.

A writer in "N. and Q.," August 10, 1850, says: "I will state a circumstance that occurred to myself about 1788. Passing in a hackney coach up the old Bailey to West Smithfield, I saw the unquenched embers of a fire opposite Newgate. On my alighting, I asked the coachman, 'What was that fire in the Old Bailey over which the wheel of your coach passed?' 'Oh, sir,' he replied, 'they have been burning a woman for murdering her husband.'"

A full account of the execution is in the "Gentleman's Magazine" for 13th March and 18th March 1789. "This is the execution at which I was present," says another writer in "N. and Q." "Eight of the malefactors suffered on the scaffold, then known as the New Drop. After they were suspended, the woman, in a white dress, was brought out of Newgate alone, and after some time spent in devotion, was hung on the projecting arm of a low gibbet, fixed at a little distance from the scaffold. After the lapse of a sufficient time to extinguish life, faggots were piled around her, and over her head, so that the person was completely covered. Fire was then set to the pile, and the woman was consumed to ashes."

In the "Gentleman's Magazine" for June 21, 1786, is the account of the burning of Phoebe Harris for counterfeiting the coin of the realm.

In Harrison's "Derby and Nottingham Journal," September 22, 1779, is an account of another such sentence: "On Saturday, two persons were capitally convicted at the Old Bailey of High Treason—viz., Isabella Condon, for coining shillings in Coldbath Fields, and John Field, for coining shillings in Nag's Head Yard, Bishopsgate Street. They will receive sentence to be drawn on a hurdle to the place of execution the woman to be burnt, and the man to be hanged."

From Angliæ Notitia, by Edward Chamberlain, LL.D., F.R.S., 1676. P. 44:—

"Petit Treason is when a servant killeth his master or mistress, or a wife killeth her husband. The punishment for a woman convicted of high treason or petit treason is all one, and that is to be drawn and burnt alive." P. 292:—"The Law allots the same punishment to a woman that shall kill her husband as to a woman that shall kill her father or master, and that is petit treason, to be burnt alive."

The Shrewsbury case was, I believe, the last in England. On May 10th, 1790, Sir Benjamin Hammett, in the House of Commons, called attention to the then state of the law. He said that it had been his painful office and duty in the previous year to attend the burning of a female, he being at the time Sheriff of London; and he moved to bring in a Bill to alter the law. He showed that the Sheriff who shrank from executing the sentence of burning alive was liable to a prosecution, but he thanked Heaven that there was not a man in England who would carry such a sentence literally into execution. The executioner was allowed to strangle the woman condemned to the stake, before flames were applied; but such an act of humanity was a violation of the law, subjecting executioner and Sheriff to penalties. The Act was passed 30 George III. C. 48.

It is a startling thought that in the time of our grandfathers such atrocities could have been permitted by law. We move so rapidly now, and the swing of the pendulum has been so greatly into the other extreme, that we forget that little over a century has elapsed since the last stake was kindled in England about the body of a wretched woman.

Sabine Baring-Gould – A Concise Bibliography

Sabine Baring-Gould's full bibliography consists of over 1200 works. Many of these are songs and hymns with the best known being 'Onward Christian Soldiers'.

A Book of the Pyrenees (1907)
Court Royal (1891)
A Book of Dartmoor (1900)
A Book of North Wales (1903)
A Book of Ghosts (1904)
A Book of South Wales (1905)
A Book of the Rhine from Cleve to Mainz (1906)
A Book of The West: Being An Introduction To Devon and Cornwall (2 Volumes, 1899)
A First Series of Village Preaching for a Year
A Garland of Country Songs (with Henry Fleetwood Sheppard) (1895)
A Second Series of Village Preaching for a Year
An Old English Home and its Dependencies, London, 1898
Arminell

Bladys of the Stewponey (1919)
Cliff Castles and Cave Dwellings of Europe
Cornish Characters (1909)
Curiosities of Olden Times (1896)
Curious Myths of the Middle Ages (1866)
Dartmoor Idylls (1896)
Devon (1907) (Methuen's Little Guide on Devonshire)
Devon Characters and Strange Events (1908)
Domitia (1898)
English Fold Songs for Schools (1907)
Eve
Family Names and their story (1910)
Grettir the Outlaw: a story of Iceland (1890)
Iceland, Its Scenes and Its Sagas
In the Roar of the Sea (1891)
In Troubadour Land: A Ramble in Provence and Languedoc (1890)
John Herring
Lives of the Saints, in sixteen volumes (1897)
Legends of the Patriarchs and Prophets (from the fall of the angels to the death of Solomon).
Mehalah, A Story of the Salt Marshes (1880)
Noemi
Old Country Life (1889)
Pabo, The Priest (1899)
Red Spider (1887)
Sermons on the Seven Last words
Sermons to Children
Songs & Ballads of the West (in 4 Volumes 1881-1891)
Songs of the West: Folksongs of Devon & Cornwall (1905)
The Book of Were-Wolves, being an account of a terrible superstition (1865)
The Broom-Squire (1896)
The Gaverocks
The Life of Napoleon Bonaparte (1908)
The Lives of the Saints – a sixteen-volume collection (1872 and 1877)
The Mystery of Suffering
The Pennycomequicks
The Preacher's Pocket
The Tragedy of the Caesars (1892)
The Village Pulpit (1886)
The Vicar of Morwenstow, being a life of Robert Stephen Hawker (1876)
Urith
Village Preaching for Saints' Days

www.ingramcontent.com/pod-product-compliance
Lightning Source LLC
Chambersburg PA
CBHW071313130626
46556CB00004B/1590